Returned

Returned © 2023 Gillian Wells.
All Rights Reserved.

No part of this book may be reproduced in any form or by any electronic or mechanical means including information storage and retrieval systems, without permission in writing from the author. The only exception is by a reviewer, who may quote short excerpts in a review.

This book is a work of fiction. Names, characters, places, and incidents either are products of the author's imagination or are used fictitiously. Any resemblance to actual persons, living or dead, events, or locales is entirely coincidental.

Printed in Australia
Cover design by Shawline Publishing Group Pty Ltd
First Printing: June 2023

Shawline Publishing Group Pty Ltd
www.shawlinepublishing.com.au

Paperback ISBN 978-1-9229-9333-5
Ebook ISBN 978-1-9229-9338-0

Distributed by Shawline Distribution and Lightningsource Global

A catalogue record for this work is available from the National Library of Australia

More great Shawline titles can be found by scanning the QR code below.
New titles also available through Books@Home Pty Ltd.
Subscribe today at www.booksathome.com.au or scan the QR code below.

Returned

GILLIAN WELLS

To everyone that was badly affected by COVID and especially those who lost loved ones. May your pain lessen as time moves on. Hopefully the world has learnt much from this episode.

To the amazing team at Shawline - with my deepest gratitude for all the help and care you have given me on my writing journey. You are all fantastic.

Chapter 1

Sally gazed at the buildings in awe. They were so old and so pretty. The nearby statue of Cyrano de Bergerac, however, was painted in garish colours, and she didn't like the look of him much.

She turned to her guide to ask him about the statue but found he'd walked on. She hurried to catch up. The street was busy with tourists, and she didn't want to lose him. With her eyes firmly fixed on his back, she walked right into a tall man, who, like her, had been looking at the buildings.

Her apology froze on her lips. She found herself gazing into the dark eyes that had invaded her dreams for so long.

'Seb,' she whispered.

'Sally!'

They stood staring at each other for a heartbeat, then their arms were about each other, as the last ten years fell away.

Seb recovered first.

'What are you doing here? How are you? You look amazing.'

She'd matured into a beautiful woman with poise and elegance. Seb, on the other hand, had deep lines around his mouth and a quiet sadness in his eyes. Although he was only thirty-one, his rich brown hair was streaked with grey.

Sally's guide, having watched their reunion, stepped forward.

'Monsieur, I am Pierre de Monfort.' He shook Seb's hand. Introductions were made, and Pierre asked how long they'd known each other and when they'd last met.

'Ten years, two months, and a few weeks ago,' said Sally.

'But this is wonderful,' Pierre said. 'Sebastian, you must join us for dinner.'

Seb opened his mouth to refuse, but seeing the pleading look on Sally's face, instead replied, 'Thank you, I'd like that. But I still don't understand. Why are you here, Sally?'

'I work for a wine import company in Sydney, and I'm visiting vineyards and finding new suppliers,' she said. 'I'm staying with Pierre and his family. But how about you? I heard you live in England now.'

'Long story. Suffice to say, I'm here because of a horse and, like you, took a sideways trip to look around Bergerac.'

After they parted, with promises to catch up properly later, Pierre was highly amused by the change in his companion. He tried to question her, but she deflected his questions and finally, he gave up. He'd noticed, however, how it was as if she'd been lit up from within. Although she'd already been lovely, now she sparkled. He'd thought before that he'd like her to be his mistress, and now he was certain of it – but he was also certain he didn't stand much of a chance after she'd met her long-lost lover. It was plain to him that was the relationship between Sally and Seb, who Pierre had to admit was extremely handsome.

Pierre had the strangest feeling he'd seen Seb before. Tall and good looking, but serious, careworn. Then, as he drove them back to his house, the penny dropped.

'Your friend,' he said, tapping his fingers on the steering wheel, 'he is some sort of horse person – a whisperer, they call him, *oui?*'

'Yes, how did you know?' Sally asked, surprised.

'A friend of mine was saying about an English man who can tame bad horses. He showed me a piece in the local paper, with a photograph, too, though I thought it was a different name.' Pierre sighed. 'My daughter, the one you haven't met, wants to be a groom of all things. She is joining us tonight. Fortunate, yes?'

'Seb's from Australia, really. Like me. He came over to England a few years ago and has never been back. He uses his middle name now – Charles, or Charlie.'

'You have kept in touch, then?'

'No, not for a long time. I just follow what he does in the horse world.'

Sally felt uncomfortable. She hoped it didn't sound as if she were stalking Seb. Sometimes, she went a year without knowledge of what he was doing.

Pierre was looking forward to an interesting evening. He was a people-watcher, as well as a romantic, and what little he'd seen and heard had sparked his imagination. Also, he thought if his daughter spent time working in stables, it might put her off her chosen career. He was hoping she'd take a position on the family vineyard. Though it could be hard, he reflected, to get her a job with this Australian, as he was so well-known he likely had a whole army of people working for him.

Chapter 2

Seb turned his hire car into Pierre's driveway, passing through a set of wrought-iron gates. He'd lived in England for the last five years but was still in awe of the grand buildings both there and across Europe, where his reputation had seen him travel. The chateau was as imposing as any he'd seen, and there were several cars parked out front. He hoped it wouldn't be a large gathering, as they were one of the things he struggled with.

Once out of the car, he took a few minutes to look around. Coming into spring, the vines lining the driveway were bare, as were the lawns and rose beds closer to the house. The stone steps leading up to the front door were bordered with daffodils, which shone bright yellow as the sun went down.

When he approached the door, it burst open. Sally stood there. Her long blonde hair was piled on top of her head, and her blue eyes were sparkling, made brighter by her navy jumper. Her jeans were tight and showed off her shapely legs.

Seb drew in a breath. She was even lovelier than he'd remembered. He'd been so surprised to see her earlier that he hadn't noticed how she'd looked – it had been her scent and her essence that he'd remembered. In some respects, he regretted accepting the invitation to dinner, as he was afraid of his feelings towards Sally. He'd broken away from her before, but could he do it again? It'd been the hardest thing he'd ever done. At times, his regrets had nearly undone him. But then, maybe she was married, or had a partner. Someone as beautiful as her couldn't still be single.

'Seb.'

She put her arms around his neck and kissed him fleetingly on the cheek. As Seb held her slender body against his, he knew he was lost again in his love for her.

A discreet cough parted them.

'Monsieur, welcome. Come and meet my family,' Pierre said, with a smile.

He led the way down a stone passage, into a small, cosy room. In the middle was a table set for dinner, with places for six. Inwardly, Seb breathed a sigh of relief.

A dark-haired woman appeared, followed by a young man so like Pierre he was plainly his son. Pierre made introductions. His wife, Margaret, was English. Their son, Louis, was friendly and open-faced; Seb liked him at once.

'How many children do you have?' Seb asked Margaret, as Pierre was getting drinks.

'Four. Two are in Paris – our other son is training to be an architect, and our eldest daughter is doing medicine.'

'What about you, Louis? What do you do?' asked Seb, accepting a glass of red from Pierre.

'I'm joining Papa in our wine business. There's a lot to learn, but—'

Louis broke off as the door slammed open and a tall woman rushed into the room. She had dark red hair, which fell in waves down her voluptuous figure, green eyes, and a full, sensuous mouth. She was one of the most beautiful women Seb had ever seen. He found himself staring at her, then Pierre stepped forward.

'Ha, you've joined us, then. Allow me to introduce my daughter,

Brianna. Brianna, this is Monsieur Proctor.'

Seb put out his hand, but she ignored it and kissed him lightly on both cheeks, French-style. Her scent made Seb think of summer flowers. She was dressed in jumper and jeans like Sally, and though her clothes were casual, they oozed class.

'Monsieur Proctor, I understand you are here to tame horses, yes?' Her voice was husky, and her English was almost accent-free.

'Yes. Though please, everyone, call me Charlie. I was here to see a couple of problem horses. I've spent a few days with them, and I'm returning to England tomorrow.' As he said this, he heard Sally draw a sharp breath.

'Couldn't you stay another day, Seb?' she asked. 'I'm not leaving until Monday. I was hoping Pierre wouldn't mind if I spent Sunday with you.'

Sally knew she sounded needy but couldn't help herself. Horrifyingly, she was already feeling jealous of Pierre's beautiful daughter.

Brianna looked confused. 'I thought your name was Charlie?'

'It is. Charles, or Charlie, is my middle name. Sally here is an old friend and knows me by my first.'

'I see. Please, tell me about these horses – I'm dying to hear all about what you do. I never thought I'd be lucky enough to meet you!'

Seb took a sip of his wine, embarrassed. He didn't like speaking about himself and always kept horse talk to a minimum while away from them. At the back of his mind, he wondered whether Pierre had had an ulterior motive in asking him to dinner.

'Later, maybe,' he said. 'I don't want to talk horses and bore everyone; I'd like to hear about the vineyard first. This is excellent wine.'

Pierre beamed. 'Now come sit, and we will eat.'

There were mini quiches to start, followed by a tossed salad, lamb chops, cheese, and a dessert. Seb felt as if he'd eaten enough food for a week. He was still careful about what and how much he ate, a habit left over from his time as a marathon runner. The wine flowed freely, though after a couple of glasses, Seb put a hand over his glass. 'I'm driving, best not.'

'*Psh,* do not worry. The police here will leave you alone,' Pierre said, ignoring Seb's wishes and filling his glass anyway.

Later, Seb found he'd unwittingly almost finished his drink. Much of the conversation was about wine, but some of it focused on Britain leaving the European Union. He could tell the family were worried, but kept quiet, as it was all a mystery to him. Horses were his entire world and he shut himself off from most other things in the news.

Sally was also quiet. She'd noticed how Brianna hung onto Seb's every word and how often his eyes strayed to Brianna. Too often, she felt.

Towards the end of the meal, Brianna asked Seb about his horses.

'I don't have many myself,' he said, 'but horses come to my yard to be trained or retrained, usually if they have a problem with their temperament.'

'Do you employ many people, then?' asked Pierre.

'I have a secretary and two full-time grooms, as well as a couple of part-timers.'

'Is that enough?' Pierre raised his eyebrows. 'Do you not want more? There is a young lady at this table who would jump at the chance to work for you.'

This was a bombshell Seb hadn't seen coming. Nor had Sally, who instinctively didn't like the idea.

Slowly, Seb shook his head. 'I'm sorry, but I don't actually need any more help just now.'

Sally let out the breath she'd been holding.

'I'll make it worth your while,' Pierre said. 'If she's not up to the job, just send her home. No hard feelings.'

Seb stared at him in disbelief. 'Are you saying you'll pay me to take her on?'

Even Brianna looked unhappy. 'Papa!' she said.

'I will be frank with you all. Brianna here is horse-mad. She has finished college, but all she wants is to be with horses. However, I want her to come into the vineyard with me and my son. Brianna, I am proposing that you work with this young man for a year. If you still want to be a groom at the end, so be it. But if you are unsure, come into our wine business without regrets. I will give you this time to make up your mind once and for all. Do we have an agreement?'

'Yes, Papa, yes!'

Brianna jumped up and hurried to hug her father.

'Excuse me, but I haven't agreed to take her yet,' Seb said, sounding rather desperate.

'You don't have to pay her,' Pierre said. 'I'll pay you. I'll make it worth your while, I promise.' He named a figure that had Seb's mind reeling.

Seb was nonplussed. How could he say no without seeming churlish? He nodded, uncomfortable.

'Do not worry, I will have a proper agreement drawn up,' Pierre said. 'Now, a glass of champagne to celebrate.'

'Not for me, I'm driving.'

'Nonsense. We have many rooms – you must stay here.'

Pierre left in search of champagne, and Seb realised he was a man used to getting his own way.

In the end, he decided it wasn't such a bad idea. So far, he'd hardly had a chance to speak with Sally. He'd spent the whole time acutely aware of her, but had hardly looked her way, because he didn't want to inflame his feelings any further.

The evening wore on, until there was only him, Pierre and Sally left. Pierre got to his feet.

'I'll leave you two to reminisce. Sally, you can show Charlie to the room next to yours. *Bonne nuit.*'

Then he too was gone.

The atmosphere was electric, but both stayed where they were, on either side of the dinner table.

Sally was first to speak. Clearing her throat, she said, 'You didn't want to take Brianna, did you?'

Without taking his eyes off her, Seb shook his head.

'She's very beautiful.' Sally tried not to sound as extremely jealous as she felt.

'Not as beautiful as you,' he said. 'Many times, I wanted to get back in touch. You've never been far from my thoughts. I was afraid I carried bad blood, but I'm not sure it works like that.' He got to his feet, muttering, 'I didn't notice Brianna in any case.' Coming around the table, he bent down and kissed her neck.

Sally turned to him, and then they were kissing as if their lives depended on it.

Pulling back, she led him up the huge staircase and into her bedroom. Remembering that frantic lovemaking had killed Seb's passion in the past, she tried to slow down. He had other ideas. Clothes were strewn about, and they fell onto the bed. There were no ghosts haunting Seb now. He made love to Sally with a passion and urgency that took them both by surprise. After climaxing together, they lay panting on the sheets.

'My God, you're so gorgeous,' he said. 'I've missed you so much.'

Tears ran down Sally's face. Her throat was too closed-up to speak.

'My darling girl, what have I done? What's wrong?'

Taking a big gulp of air, Sally managed to say, 'Nothing. I just love you so much... I never thought I'd see you again. That was so wonderful – better than my wildest dreams.'

'There's more where that came from,' Seb said, leaning over to kiss her again. 'Much more.'

This time, they took it slowly, enjoying each other's bodies. The night passed with little sleep and a lot of love.

Towards dawn, they finally talked of the intervening years. They'd both had short flings with others, but never anything that'd lasted. Sally had worked for a few smaller wine companies in and around Sydney, gone to South Australia for a time, then returned to New South Wales.

Seb had gone to counselling, but horses had really saved him. Gradually, they'd become his life. He had an almost magical affinity with them, and after a time, he'd relocated to the UK, where there was more call for his expertise. In some ways, he'd found it healing to get away from Australia. But he'd been away for five years now, and he hadn't seen any of his family since his parents made one short trip over soon after he'd moved.

'Maybe I could think about moving back, if you want me to,' he said.

'Need you ask?' Sally kissed him lightly. 'Now we've found each other again, please stay in my life. I couldn't bear to lose you a second time.'

Seb felt the same way. 'I guess we've wasted enough time as it is... and that's all my fault.'

'Don't say that. You needed the time, and I think we've both benefitted from it. We were so young, but now we're older and wiser.'

'You remember my sisters? Sarah's a doctor now, and Caitlin has two children. I'd like to see my niece and nephew.'

They talked and talked, catching up on the last ten years. Hearing Sally talk of her job in the countryside and what she did on her days off, Seb felt an overwhelming wave of homesickness. He was ready to go back. However, it would take some months to organise. He had a full schedule, and he'd have to either sell the four horses he owned or take them to Australia. Mist, the grey Arab mare who'd saved him, had passed away five years ago. It was one of the things that'd made him decide to leave. Now, it was time to return.

Chapter 3

They were both late for breakfast. They'd slept through their alarms, then showered together, which had of course delayed things even more. Then, Seb had managed to change his flight until Tuesday, as he needed to get his head around taking on Brianna, who'd be flying back to England with him.

When they appeared in the dining room, Pierre smiled and couldn't resist asking if they'd had a good night. He was highly amused to see conflicting thoughts pass across their faces.

'I hope you didn't let this beautiful woman sleep all alone!' he said, much to their embarrassment.

Seb took Sally with him when he went to pay his bill at his little hotel. He'd stay at Pierre's chateau until his flight home.

'What would you like to do now, Sal?' Seb asked, as he held the door open for her, and she followed him out onto the sun-bathed street.

'Walk along the banks of the river. Talk, sit, eat, drink. Ordinary things that'll be extraordinary because I'm doing them with you. I still can't quite believe we're here together... it's like magic.' She clasped her hands together. 'How long before you can come back to Australia? Will you come back? You said last night you'd been thinking of it. Do you still want to?'

'Now I've found you again, yes. It'd been on my mind for some time, and seeing you again has confirmed it. Hopefully, the move won't take me too long – I keep hearing about this Covid-19 thing, this pandemic. I'm worried it'll make life difficult.'

'I've been so busy I haven't taken much notice, and my French isn't good enough to understand it all. I do know there have been a lot of deaths in Italy, and some people have it here, but it all seems far away.'

'Let's hope it'll have died down by the time I get to Australia. It's the first of March today – the first day of autumn back home. I probably won't make it over until late winter, or even spring. I own the yard in England, and I have the horses to find homes for. I'd bring them back with me, but it would be very expensive, and I know of two people who'd like to buy them anyway. I also have commitments I must fill – workshops and training sessions. It wouldn't be fair to leave people in the lurch. I won't take any more bookings, though! We've got through ten years apart. Now we know we'll be together, so we'll just have to be patient a short time, then—'

Seb stopped walking. Looking at Sally intensely, he said, 'Live with me. Say you'll stay with me, Sal. Please.'

Sally gasped. 'I... I didn't expect you to say that!'

Seb smiled. 'Nor did I. I just want to be with you, live with you, not only see you sometimes.'

'Yes, Seb. Yes, yes. But what about Brianna? You promised you'd take her on for a year.'

'Well, she can come to Australia too. It'll be good for her to experience the world out there, and I'm sure her father won't mind.'

'Mm.' Sally sounded sceptical.

'Sal, I know you think she'll turn my head because she's beautiful, but I love you. I've met many attractive women while we've been away from each other. Some of them... let's just say, if I were interested, they wouldn't have minded. I've had a few flings too, as I told you, but that's all they were. I've loved you nonstop for ten years. You don't need to worry.'

'I know, I'm being silly. I'll shut up now.'

Seb shut her up anyway by kissing her thoroughly.

They had a wonderful day together, ending with another lovely meal at Pierre's chateau. Pierre again broke out the champagne when told of their plans. Seb, uncharacteristically, had announced the news during dinner. Normally so quiet and serious, he was the life and soul of the evening. Sally had hardly ever seen him so full of joy. It was like he'd been lit up from within. His beautiful brown eyes sparkled, and he seemed to sit straighter, taller. He charmed them all.

That night, he said it was as if a mantle of gloom had been lifted from his shoulders. Little did they know, it was about to descend again, lower and blacker than ever.

Chapter 4

It was a tearful goodbye the next morning, but Seb and Sally told themselves and each other they'd be back together soon. They were both rather weary, as again, they hadn't had much sleep the night before. They didn't care.

Seb phoned his parents to tell them the news. They were amazed he'd met Sally again and overjoyed he was coming home. His mother, Connie, told him she'd get in touch with Joan, Sally's mother. 'We'll have the party to end all parties,' she said.

Joan was also very pleased when Sally called her. She knew her daughter's heart had broken when Seb had ended their relationship. Now, Joan lived in Queensland – her husband had passed away two years before from a massive heart attack, and she'd moved to be closer to Sally's brother, who worked on the Sunshine Coast.

Seb spent the rest of Monday with Brianna and her father. Pierre was very thorough in all his business dealings and wanted to make sure Seb completely understood what was required of him, as well as what Seb could expect from him and Brianna.

'So,' Seb said, 'when I finally get everything sorted out, you're happy for Brianna to come to Australia with me?'

'Of course, it will be good for her,' Pierre said.

'I'm slightly worried by all this talk about a pandemic, but hopefully it won't impact us too much.'

'I think it will have fizzled out in a few months' time. Look at SARS – that never became the big thing they said it would.'

The next day, everything being in place, Brianna and Seb set off to England. Brianna had been many times to visit her grandparents, but this was different. She was bubbling with excitement. They both felt uneasy, though, when they saw quite a few people wearing face masks.

'Funny to think we're in England now,' Brianna mused, as they clambered into Seb's Discovery, which he'd left at the airport. 'A short time ago, we were in France. And Sally, who left yesterday, isn't home yet.'

Brianna hadn't been to the Essex-Suffolk border, where they were headed. It was colder, and the vegetation was still grey and dead. The day was overcast. She gave an involuntary shiver, and Seb glanced across at her.

'Are you okay?'

'Yes,' she said. 'Someone walked over my grave, as they say.'

'I hate that expression.'

Brianna laughed. 'I hadn't really thought about it before. I suppose it is rather creepy.'

Although it was modest compared to her family home, and not at its best, given the time of year, Brianna was enchanted by Seb's place. It was an old farmhouse, rendered in pink plaster, with tall chimneys and large windows. Behind the house was a yard lined with stables. A gate at the other end led out to the training grounds. Its white-painted fences could be seen through the archway as they drew up behind the house.

Getting out of the car, Seb said, 'I'll show you your room. You'll be sharing the staff flat with two others. Here they come – let me introduce you.'

Brianna had already been told she'd be sharing but had imagined it'd be in the main house, not in a unit over the stables.

Marjorie was an older woman with a weather-beaten face and a kind smile. 'Call me Marj, everyone does.'

'I'm Helen. Difficult to shorten that,' said the other woman, who Brianna guessed was in her late twenties.

'We'll show Brianna her room, Boss,' Marj said.

'Alright, but I need to speak to you both as soon as you've done that. Meet me in the office.'

The two women nodded, looking mystified. Brianna knew what Seb was going to say to them but had been told to keep quiet.

'Do you always call him Boss?' she asked, as they went upstairs to the flat, which ran nearly the whole length of the yard.

'Yes. It's respectful, and he likes it,' Helen said. 'Mr Proctor is too formal, and Charlie too familiar.'

'How long have you worked here?'

'I've been here two years, Marj four and a bit. He's a good man – kind, considerate and fair. Work hard and you'll be rewarded. We've had some real nutcase horses, but he's amazing with them. He turns them into quite special animals. However, he can be very serious, and we both think he's troubled sometimes. You can see it in his eyes and face. We don't know his history, or how you met him. We didn't know he was intending on hiring more staff, either.'

'I think you need to hear what Char— sorry, Boss – has to say. He'll tell you what you want to know.'

They entered a large, comfortable living area, lit by massive windows, with sofas and a big TV. Further in were a dining table and chairs, and a well-appointed kitchen. To the right was a series of doors.

Marj led Brianna into a small but cosy bedroom. 'Bathroom's just next door,' she said. 'We'd better go and see what this is all about. Are you coming too?'

'No, I know what you're going to hear. I'll unpack, if that's alright with you.'

'Sure,' Helen said. 'You won't meet Jean yet. She's the secretary, but only works part-time. She'll be in tomorrow.' Both women were secretly unimpressed Brianna knew more than they did, but didn't show it.

The office was just through the back door of the main house. Seb was waiting, sitting at his desk. Though neither Marj nor Helen mentioned it until afterwards, they were both struck by the notion that he looked different.

He indicated the chairs against the wall. 'Sit down, you two. Now, this is a bit of a bombshell, but I'm selling up and returning to Australia – no, wait, hear me out.'

Both women had started to speak at once, looking horror-struck.

'I'm hoping to do much the same thing there, and I'm inviting you both to come, should you wish to. This has all happened very suddenly, but I met a woman I've loved for many years quite by chance, and we're planning on being together. Brianna's father has invested in my business, so she'll come to Australia too. She has a year's contract. We'll see how she shapes up. Her father was there when I met Sally, the woman I just told you about, and she can fill in any gaps that she knows. We'll complete any commitments we have here over the next few months. It'll take time to sell this place and the horses I own, as I'm not planning on taking them. Like I said, you've both been loyal to me, and I'd be very happy if you wished to throw in your lots with me and come to Australia. If you want to stay in England, I'll give you excellent references. Now, go away and think about it. It won't be an easy decision.'

Marj and Helen were silent as they walked back to their quarters. It was lunchtime, so on autopilot, they started to prepare food. Brianna came out of her room and saw their bewildered expressions.

'Charlie's told you, then? What will you do?'

'We haven't had time to think yet,' snapped Marj.

'Sorry, of course not. I've only just met him, but over these past few days, he's changed – become lighter, somehow. When he told us he and Sally were going to be together, I don't think I've ever seen anyone happier. He was glowing.'

Helen looked at Brianna for several long moments, then said, 'You're right. I think we were both so caught up in everything else, but he has changed, almost overnight. He always seemed sad before, even when he was laughing. I always felt he'd been through something horrible. I don't know what, but I'm guessing he's had a hard time at some point.'

'Well, we've certainly got something to think about,' Marj said. 'Come on, Brianna. Tuck in, then we'll show you round and tell you what's expected of you.'

'Yes, Charlie said the day-to-day running was in your hands.' Brianna took the plate of sandwiches they'd made, and the three of them sat at the table. The talk turned to horses. Brianna had always had a passion for the animals, and her father had indulged it. She'd owned her own horse and had competed in one-day events, though Pierre had insisted she sold it before she went to university. When she'd returned home, she'd been lost without a horse. There had been a few heated exchanges between her and her father. Now, she'd got her own way – at least for the moment.

Aside for the horses Seb owned, there were only three in the stables, though two more were arriving the next day. All were problem horses in some way, but Marj told Brianna that no horses ever left the place without being cured.

'Like the boss always says, humans are usually to blame for a horse's behavioural problems,' Marj said, as she and Brianna walked to the stables. 'Sometimes, it's bred into them – you get a cranky mare, and she'll make her offspring cranky. That doesn't happen often, though.'

One horse caught Brianna's attention: a beautiful, almost-black Arab gelding, who was standing at the back of his loose box, ignoring them.

'Who's this?' she asked.

'He has a long Arabic name, but we call him Goblin. He just arrived yesterday and is here to be retrained – he doesn't like humans much. Boss hasn't seen him yet.'

'Is this him, then?' a voice asked behind them.

Seb had come across without them noticing. He opened the door, as Marj said, 'They told me he'll kick if you're a stranger. He didn't like us feeding him this morning or mucking out. Took us ten minutes to put his headcollar on so we could clean the stall.'

'Are you frightened, then?' Seb moved slowly into the loose box. His voice was soft. 'Poor boy. Come and say hello.' He stopped a little way from the door and held his hand out, palm-up.

Goblin, who was standing parallel to the wall, turned his head. His ears flicked back and forth as Seb continued to speak in a gentle voice. Slowly, he took a step towards Seb, then another. Stretching out his head, he delicately sniffed Seb's palm. Seb put his hand up and stroked his nose. He visibly relaxed. Minutes later, Seb was running his hands all over his neck and back, and he looked as if he was half asleep.

'That's the boss's magic at work,' Marj said quietly to Brianna.

'Wow,' breathed Brianna. 'I've never seen anything like it.'

'You'll see lots more in the weeks to come. He's a magician – I'm still amazed every time I see it.'

'I think I'll enjoy it here,' Brianna said.

Chapter 5

Sally found the trip back to Australia frustrating. She just wanted to get there and start planning. In the past, she'd made the trip to Europe a few times and had vaguely thought about visiting England and looking Seb up, but had always chickened out. Now, she thought it was better this way. He'd largely laid his demons to rest, it seemed. Although they hadn't talked too much about the long-term future yet, she didn't care. Seb by her side was all she wanted.

She lived in Sydney, but Seb had said he wanted to live in Queensland, near his family. As hers were now there, it sounded perfect. Once she knew when he was coming, she'd hand in her notice and start looking for a place for them both. She was bubbling with joy, though seeing the news on the plane had her a little worried. There was talk of lockdowns due to the virus that seemed to be travelling the world. The number of deaths in some countries was alarming. A small shiver of fear ran down her spine.

The press always make things worse than they are, she reassured herself. *And the authorities are probably panicking too.*

When she finally got to her apartment, she found several messages on her answerphone, which surprised her, as she had her mobile with her at all times. They were mostly scam calls, though the oldest was from an ex-boyfriend who was now just a friend and a fully qualified doctor. He sounded stressed, and asked Sally to ring him as soon as she got the message. Sally looked at the time – 9.30 in the morning. She wasn't due back to the office until the fifth, which was Thursday. She was always so jetlagged that she usually gave herself a day or so to recover. She tried her ex's number, but it went straight to voicemail. She realised he couldn't call her mobile, as she'd changed her number since she'd last seen him, due to her phone being stolen a few months back.

After having a quick shower, she drove to the supermarket. It was a large place with a big car park, and she was surprised to find it heaving, people streaming out of the shops with trolleys laden with toilet rolls. How could that be? What was going on? When she went inside, she couldn't find any spare trolleys, so she went back out. Finding a woman loading her car with toilet rolls and flour and meat, Sally asked if she could have her trolley when she'd finished.

'What's going on?' Sally asked.

The woman gave her a pitying look. 'Where have you been, love? Haven't you heard we're all going to suffer from this virus? We won't be able to buy anything. I think the world's coming to an end. I want to make sure I have enough to keep my family going.'

Sally looked at the huge mountain of toilet rolls, then back at the woman. 'It'll take a while to use all that.'

The woman turned aggressive. 'Don't find fault with me! A lot of people are taking more stuff. You'd better hurry – there isn't much left.' With that, she pushed the trolley into Sally and got in her car, grumbling to herself.

Sally wasn't hurt, but the woman had annoyed her. There was no need for all that. And why toilet paper?

However, when she got into the store, it was mayhem. People pushed and shoved, arguing over toilet paper and flour. Meat was disappearing too; many shelves were empty. Thankfully,

Sally didn't want toilet paper, as by the time she got there, the shelves were empty. She wanted fruit, vegetables, meat and cheese, but there was hardly anything left. It was far worse than Christmas. Finally, she abandoned her trolly and took herself to a delicatessen a little further away. It was expensive, so she only went there on special occasions. They were short of stock too, but she managed to get most things she needed. By the time she got home, she was exhausted.

After putting her purchases away, she went to her bed. She'd only just lain down when her landline went. She considered just letting it ring, then thought better of it.

'Sally, I'm glad to get hold of you. You've been away – France, wasn't it?'

It was Christopher Lane, her ex. He sounded very unlike himself.

'Yes, hello. What's going on, Chris?'

'Well, I've been worried about you. Europe has so many cases of the virus, and I think it's pretty serious. I want you to get tested, to make sure you're alright.'

'Don't be silly. I'm fine, never better. In fact, I'm blooming.' A gurgle of excitement raced through Sally's veins. She'd only told her mother and brother, and now was the chance to tell someone else. 'I just met the man I want to spend the rest of my life with,' she blurted.

Silence, then Christopher said, 'When? Who? But you were away.'

'I've always loved him, Chris. That's why I couldn't commit to you, or anyone else. I met him in France quite by chance, and we... well, we got together again. He's the horse whisperer I think I mentioned before.'

'I see. Is he Australian, then, or French?'

'Australian. But what's the panic? You really rang me about having a test?'

'Yes, Sally. This virus is a killer, and so many people aren't taking it seriously. Please have a test to make sure you're okay. You'll have to isolate if you have it. It's not mandatory yet, but soon all travellers coming from overseas will have to isolate for fourteen days.'

'Jesus!' Sally didn't often swear, but this shook her. She'd been so taken up with her time in France, meeting Seb, that she'd been living in a kind of golden bubble. The shopping trip, and now this... it was a big wake-up call.

Finally, Sally promised she'd get tested if she felt at all unwell. When she put the phone down, she looked at the time. It was the middle of the night in England. She'd wake Seb up, if she called him now. Would he mind?

Suddenly, the urge to cry overcame her. She wasn't normally an emotional person, but the last few days in France, followed by this bizarre homecoming, had taken their toll. She snatched up the phone and punched in his number before she chickened out.

'Yes?'

Seb had been in a deep sleep. The phone's ringing had startled him, leaving his heart racing. He'd immediately thought of his dad, who'd suffered a brain tumour ten years before.

'Seb, I'm sorry I woke you, but... but...' Sally was having trouble containing her tears.

'Darling girl, whatever is the matter?'

'I'm overreacting, I know, but the supermarket was bare, and they're talking about lockdowns and Covid tests, and I miss you!'

'I think you might be overtired from your trip. Having said that, the world does seem to have gone mad, these last few days. It's the same here – supermarket shelves stripped of toilet rolls. Why toilet rolls?' He laughed softly. 'I was expecting more horses, but the owners are holding back because we may have a lockdown here. There's hardly enough work for the four of us now that Brianna's come too.'

Calmed by the sound of Seb's laugh, Sally sighed, her chest lightening. 'Will you be okay?'

'Sure. I'd be better if you were here, though. Just hearing your voice has made me want you rather badly. Not much more sleep for me... unless you could come here and relieve my problem.'

Sally giggled. 'I'm standing here in the nude, and I have an ache that needs something hard to massage it away.'

Seb groaned. 'Have a little mercy on me. I'm in agony, here.'

After a few more minutes, they reluctantly hung up. Apart from the fact Sally's needs were heightened, she felt much better – and later, when she went to bed, she slept soundly.

Chapter 6

Time marched on. Covid-19 was almost the sole topic of conversation around the world, as people struggled with the restrictions imposed by jittery governments worried about how their health systems and financial institutes would cope. The Western world shut down. Streets were bare, supermarkets were the only shops open, and postmen were inundated with online shopping orders.

Then, a new worry reared its head: mental health, especially that of people in high-rise buildings, those who lived alone, and the elderly. Some said the virus was a conspiracy and wasn't real at all – though it was a mystery how they thought that when people were dying left, right and centre.

Seb was worried about his business. At first, it hadn't been so bad. He'd retrained the horses that were already in the stables, and he'd been able to return all of them except for Goblin, whose owners were overseas. Then the consultancy part of his business dried up completely. Finally, he made a decision and called Helen into the office.

'Look, I'm very sorry, but I can't keep you on,' he said. 'There isn't enough for the three of you to do now the business has stopped. Heaven knows when I'll get back to Australia. Could you find another job? Jean finished yesterday, as you know – she was thinking of retiring in any case.'

Helen was very upset but tried not to show it, knowing none of it was within Seb's control. A few days later, partly thanks to the excellent reference Seb had given her, she had another job, working at a racing stable in Newmarket. The racehorses still needed looking after.

Sally's job as wine buyer took a different turn. She couldn't go out and about, so she worked from home, helping with the sudden increase in sales. She and Seb spoke every day, both desperate to be together again, especially as they'd just found each other after so long apart.

One day, Sally woke up early in the morning and was sick. Very sick. She couldn't keep anything down until the evening, when she suddenly felt better. Hungry, even. However, she was careful about what she ate.

The next day, the same thing happened. She was sick again, and felt fine by the evening, though drained from throwing up. She also started to cough and sneeze. By that point, she was very worried. She didn't tell Seb, but rang her mother, who immediately told her to go and get a Covid test.

There was a testing centre close to where she lived, but when she arrived, she was horrified to find she'd have to wait in line for at least a couple of hours. It was midday, and she was feeling very rough. After twenty minutes, she came over faint. The people around her moved away, thinking she had the virus, then changed their minds when she fell in a heap.

'Call an ambulance!' said a young man kneeling by Sally. He'd had some first aid training, but this was his first real patient. He checked her pulse and put her in the recovery position.

Sally's eyelids flickered. Pulling her mask to one side, she dry-heaved, pale and sweating. By now, the young man was rather worried. All his training had fled from his mind. There was this beautiful woman lying here, and he couldn't think about anything else he could do.

It took a long time for the ambulance to arrive. In the meantime, Sally recovered a little and tried to sit up, but the man wouldn't let her. 'Just stay still,' he said. 'An ambulance is on its way.'

'I don't need an ambulance. It's just a tummy bug.'

'Well, we called one anyway – you can't be too careful.'

The ambulance arrived, and the paramedics took over. Despite Sally's protests, they whipped her off to hospital.

Three hours later, she found herself back in her apartment, feeling dazed and shocked. She rang Seb with shaking hands. It was now the second time she'd called him in the middle of his night.

'Sal, what's up?' He'd already been awake, worrying about selling up in the middle of a pandemic.

Sally burst into tears. At first, she couldn't say anything. Seb waited until she'd stopped sobbing.

'What is it, darling? Is it your mother? What's wrong?'

'Oh, Seb – promise you won't be angry, but I... I'm pregnant.'

'Jesus.'

There was a very long silence. Sally waited, sniffing. She knew him well enough to let him gather his thoughts.

'How come?' he finally asked. 'I thought you were on the pill.'

'I was – I *am* – but I had a bad tummy a couple of days before we met again. The doctor thinks that's why it didn't work. Besides, we did indulge in rather a lot of sex. Seb, I'm so sorry. I know having children was one of the things you wanted to avoid at all costs. I'll have an abortion if you want me to.'

'Sally, let me think. I need to get my head around this... it's one hell of a shock. I'll call you back.'

He hung up, and Sally sat staring at the phone. She felt ill and tired, and didn't know what to think or do. In the end, she lay on her bed, her mind in turmoil.

Half an hour later, Seb rang.

'What do you want, Sal? Do you want to keep this baby, given my ancestry?'

Sally chose her words carefully. Although it'd come as a shock, she'd always known if she ever got pregnant with Seb's child – or anyone's, for that matter – she would want it.

'Yes. I've always wanted to have a baby, and it's part of my commitment to you. When you told me you would never want children, my heart broke. It's part of why I gave in when you ended it. But now I've found you, I realise you're the most important person in my life, and I never want to be without you again. So, if you want me to have an abortion, I will. I couldn't bear losing you a second time.'

Having managed that little speech, Sally started to sob again. She was so caught up in crying that it took her a few moments to realise Seb was speaking.

'Please, please don't cry,' he said. 'I can't do anything to make you feel better from here. I want to hold you and cuddle you and make you better. When's the little Proctor due?'

'It would be in November, if... if ...'

'I should be back to see him born, then.'

'Seb, do you mean it? You don't mind?'

'Now that it's happened, I'm thrilled. I never expected to be – well, I never expected to be a dad, but now I wish I was there with you to celebrate. Believe me, I'm excited. How are you? Do you feel okay? Is everything alright? You must be careful, and make sure you have a good diet, and—'

'Seb, I'll look after myself, I promise! Let's video call later. I'm sorry I woke you, but I was beside myself. I feel so much better having talked to you. I'm going to ring Mum now.'

'I'll call my folks too. I don't think I'll get back to sleep for a while, in any case. Oh, Sal, I love you so much – I don't think I've ever been this happy.'

Sally's eyes flooded with tears. She remembered the broken man she'd loved for so long and compared him to the strong, wonderful person Seb was now.

'Love you too, darling,' she said. 'We'll speak again soon.'

A few minutes later, she was on the phone to her mother. Joan had been rather anxious when Sally had rung from France and told her she'd met Seb again. Though Joan had been glad they planned to be together, she'd been worried that Seb would break Sally's heart again. Now, when she heard the happiness in her daughter's voice and heard what Seb had said, she breathed a sigh of relief. Perhaps, in the dark days of the pandemic, things would work out well after all.

After speaking to Sally, Joan rang Connie, Seb's mother, but the line was engaged. She tried again shortly afterwards and got through.

'Hello,' Joan said. 'You've heard the news?'

'Yes, I was about to ring you. Seb was so excited that it was quite the job to get a word in, and we talked for ages. He said it was a total shock, but when he was confronted with it, he found he was so happy. I think he surprised himself!'

The two expectant grandmothers chatted for a time. When Joan had moved to live on the Sunshine Coast, Sally had given her Connie's phone number, worried about her mother having no friends in Queensland. It'd taken a while, but when Joan had plucked up the courage to call, the two women had hit it off straight away. They'd met a couple of times in Brisbane for lunch, though it wasn't something either of them could do often, as parking was expensive and they were both time-poor. Instead, they spoke on the phone occasionally. Joan had always been careful to avoid talking about Seb, though she'd told Connie what

Sally was up to. Connie had also never mentioned Seb, so his and Sally's reunion had been a big surprise to them both. Connie hadn't known Seb was going to France, as he tended to flit to Europe fairly often. Neither of them had ever thought about the two of them meeting by chance.

'Well, this is even more of a shock!' Joan said. 'Their sharing a home was amazing enough. I gather it wasn't planned?'

'No, not at all,' said Connie. 'I don't know how much Sally's told you over the years, but Seb was too scared of perpetuating bad blood, as he put it. He didn't want to have children.'

'I knew, with what Sally told me at the time. And, of course, everything that happened with your family was in the press. I've never spoken to you about it, as I was sure you wouldn't want it dragged up again.'

Connie was quiet for a short while, then she said, 'Seb had a very bad time, even worse than mine. How close relatives could behave like that is beyond comprehension. Seb's always been afraid there was something in his makeup that would come out if he fathered children. Now that it's happened, he's over the moon, and I'm sure that baby will be fine. My father, who was the root of the problem, had a very abusive upbringing. With love and care, it'll be okay, like the professionals have always told us. Seb just didn't want to take the risk.'

'I'm going to suggest that Sally move up here as soon as possible,' Joan said. 'She has friends in Sydney but no family.'

'They've closed the borders to everyone except for residents… it's going to be harder for Seb to get back. Everyone will be jumping on a plane.'

They talked a little more than rang off, agreeing to speak again soon.

The next morning, Sally jerked awake. She'd been sleeping deeply for the last hour, after a very restless night. Her mobile was ringing.

'Sal, I've been thinking... marry me, please? I don't think our baby will have tainted blood like I was afraid of. I'll explain later when I see you. Please let it be soon.'

Sally sat bolt upright in bed, her heart swelling with joy.

'I never thought you had bad blood, but I was too young to have a coherent argument,' she said. 'Yes, yes, yes to marriage.'

Chapter 7

Everyone was finding it a strange time. Seb's father Alec's work had nearly dried up. Alec's parents, who'd been travelling the country, were stuck in Western Australia, just across the border from South Australia. Seb's sister Caitlin already had two children, but the fact that Seb was to be a father had excited the family, because of all that had happened in the past. They felt Seb might be mending at last.

Caitlin's children were still small. She'd had them close together, as she was sure it was better that way. They were a girl and a boy. Emma was two, and little Alec, named after his grandfather, was only a few months old. Her husband Bob was working in the mines, so his job hadn't been affected too much by the lockdowns. He just couldn't travel when he had time off. Sarah, Seb's other sister, was a doctor on the front lines. It worried all the Proctors, even though she said she was well protected.

Back in England, with only five horses to look after and three people to do it, Seb and his employees soon found they had an excess of time on their hands. Seb knew it was no good trying to sell up under the circumstances. He decided that if he could find homes for the horses, he'd rent out his property until things settled and he could find a buyer. It was also plain that Brianna would have to return to France, while Marj would remain in England. Nothing was going the way they'd planned. His worry about returning to Australia had completely overtaken his thoughts;

getting a flight back was going to be very difficult. Then Goblin's owner, Clifford, called to say he'd managed to get back from the Middle East and was coming to collect his horse.

Clifford turned up a couple of days later. He was into endurance racing and was full of stories about where he'd been and what he'd seen. Big, bold and full of bluster, he was exactly the sort of person Seb disliked. They hadn't met before, as Goblin had been brought by Clifford's groom, and Seb had been in France. They'd only ever spoken on the phone, but Seb had already guessed Goblin's problems had been caused by his owner.

'Come into my office, and we'll settle up,' Seb said. 'He's been here quite a long time, so the bill is rather large, I'm afraid.'

When he handed it to Clifford, the man's face went puce.

'I'm not paying this. It's monstrous!'

'If you look closely, you'll see everything is itemised. Goblin has been with us ten weeks now. In addition to being retrained, he had to be fed, exercised and cared for.'

'It wasn't *my* fault I couldn't get here sooner!'

Brianna, walking across the yard, was alarmed by Clifford's shouts.

'Well, it certainly wasn't mine, either,' Seb replied. 'That is what you owe. I'm sorry if it's a shock, but I have a business to run, and I've been as fair as I can. I could actually charge more – I haven't included the price of the new rug I bought him, as the one he came with was falling to pieces.'

Clifford opened his mouth to protest further but was overcome by a coughing fit. Seb automatically took a step back. By the time Clifford had recovered, he'd forgotten to be angry and paid up, grumbling.

'That's a nasty cough. Have you seen a doctor or had a test?' Seb asked, as they walked back across the yard. Marj was waiting to load Goblin into the horsebox.

'Nah, I can't be bothered with all that nonsense. Don't believe half of what they say. Load of rubbish, I reckon.'

Goblin laid his ears back as Clifford approached him, but that was all. Moments later, he was loaded up and on his way. Seb watched the departing vehicle with a frown.

'Poor old Goblin,' said Marj. 'I feel sorry for him.'

'So do I, but we can't do anything about it. Goblin's his horse.' Seb shrugged. It wasn't the first time he'd had a difficult customer.

Back in the office, Seb wiped down everything Clifford had touched. He'd drummed caution into Marj and Brianna, making them wear masks whenever they went into the village. The man clearly hadn't been well. Seb just hoped he hadn't got the virus and passed it on.

Ten days later, his worst fears were realised. Marj announced she wasn't well and took herself off for a test. She had quite a long drive in front her, as there were no testing stations nearby. Brianna also felt peaky. Seb was pretty sure they had the virus, and that evening, he started to feel unwell too.

Brianna was the least affected. The next morning, she fed the horses alone. When she went to see Seb, she couldn't find him. With racing heart, she climbed the stairs and found him in bed. He was having trouble speaking and even struggling to breathe. She brought him some water, then raced back downstairs to tell Marj, who wasn't at all well herself.

'Best thing to do is call an ambulance,' Marj said.

Brianna did just that, only to be told it'd be quite a long wait, as they were run off their feet. She tried the doctor's surgery, but the line seemed permanently engaged. Panicking, she went back to Seb, and found him sitting on the edge of the bed. His laboured breathing frightened her.

'I'm taking you to hospital,' she said, picking up his dressing gown. Seb shook his head, then gave in, letting her help him into it.

Just then, his mobile rang on his bedside table. Brianna snatched it up.

'*Oui?*'

'Oh,' came Sally's voice, after a slight pause. 'What's going on?'

'Brianna here. The boss, he is so ill, I take to hospital.' In her panic, Brianna was speaking an odd mixture of French and English.

'What? Brianna—'

'I go now, will call you.'

Brianna hung up. Seb's eyes were on her. She didn't know how much he'd understood, but he didn't try to speak.

It took her a long time to get him downstairs and into his car. They were both exhausted by the time they'd made it. She rested her head on her arms for a minute. Her own breathing was getting strained, and she felt more ill than she ever had in her life. Luckily, she knew the way to the nearest town and went straight to its little clinic. She ran in when she got there, and before long, Seb was on his way to a major hospital, where he went straight into the ICU.

Brianna was told to go home and rest, and she wouldn't have been allowed in to see him in any case. She drove back very slowly. Her head was aching, and she was shivering so much that she had trouble holding onto the steering wheel. As she parked, the horses popped into her mind. She'd fed them that morning, but that was all. Their stables needed to be cleaned. They had to be given hay and put out in the paddock. How was she going to get all that done?

Marj was staggering across the yard, carrying a large hay net. In between coughing fits, she told Brianna she planned to put the horses in the indoor school, give them plenty of hay and leave them to it.

'Neither of us are well enough to be mucking out stables,' Marj said. 'We can put it all to rights once we feel better. Let's hope the boss makes it. From what you've told me, he's in a bad state.'

Brianna eyes filled with tears. 'He is. So bad, so bad. I have to call Sally, his partner. She rang earlier.'

'It's the middle of the night there.'

'I promised I would.'

Marj looked on the edge of collapse herself, so Brianna sent her off to bed. Although it took a long time, she managed to get the horses organised by herself, before going to the main house and finding Seb's mobile.

Sally had been waiting by her phone. It'd been so hard. She'd wanted to ring Brianna and ask what was happening, but she trusted Brianna to call back as soon as possible. She must've dozed off, because her ringtone startled her, and for a moment she didn't know where she was or what had happened.

'Hello, is that Brianna?'

'*Oui*. I managed to get the boss into hospital, and they'll look after him. He has the virus. He's very sick, but he's strong, so you mustn't worry.'

'Oh, God, no!'

'It'll be fine, I'm sure. I'll let you know how he is, and I'll give you the hospital's number, so you can ring them too.'

Brianna could hear Sally crying but could do little to help. After a few platitudes, she ended the call, promising to speak to Sally again soon. She had a shower, then crept into bed. She didn't think she'd ever felt so tired, achey and uncomfortable, and couldn't imagine how she'd get through the next few days. She hoped Marj would feel better soon. At least she didn't have to worry about the horses for a while.

Sally was beside herself. She couldn't lose Seb now, after all this time without him. She just couldn't. He'd been so excited to be a father. Now, it was possible he might die? It didn't bear thinking about. Middle of the night or not, she needed her mother.

'Sal, what's wrong? Is it the baby?'

All Joan could hear was Sally sobbing into the phone. She wasn't someone who cried easily, so Joan was doubly worried when she heard Sally so distressed.

Finally, Sally managed to speak. 'It's Seb – he's in the ICU. He's so ill. Mum, what will I do if he dies? I couldn't cope with it. I'd die too!'

Joan took a deep breath. 'Now, listen to me, Sally Macpherson. That's silly talk. If Seb is in intensive care, he's in the best place for him. It doesn't mean he's going to die. He's a young, fit man. He might be ill now, but he'll get over it. You must concentrate on taking care of your baby. Getting so upset won't be good for him or her. You're past the danger time for miscarriages, but that doesn't mean it can't happen. Now, how would you feel if you got so upset you lost this baby? What would Seb think?'

Joan's words brought Sally up with a jolt. Her mother was right; getting hysterical wouldn't help anyone. She gulped.

'Sorry, Mum. I wasn't thinking of this little one.'

The next morning, Sally just got to the phone when it rang. She picked it up, her heart racing. Was it bad news?

'Sally, love, how are you this morning?' her mother asked.

'I'm much better, thanks. Still worried out of my life, but better.'

'Why don't you move up near me, or even stay in my house for the time being? I know we talked about you coming here later, but I think the sooner you do it, the better.'

'Well, I can't, can I? The borders are shut.'

'As soon as they open, then. Or maybe you could get dispensation?'

'I'd have to talk to my boss. I'm working from home now, but as soon as the lockdown finishes, they'll expect me back.'

'Do you not want to come up here?'

'No, Mum, it's a great idea. I'd be there when Seb gets back, too... if he ever does.'

'He will, sweetheart. We just have to be patient and get through this. As they keep saying, we're all in this together.'

'I don't feel that way at all. It's like we're living in different countries, with these border shutdowns. I feel cut off. From you, from Seb, from everything. It's horrible, and it makes me sick when they roll out those platitudes.'

'They're doing their best to keep us safe, darling.'

'Physically, maybe. But what about mentally? It's harming a lot of people.'

When Joan put her phone down a few minutes later, she was extremely worried. Her daughter was usually so positive and upbeat. This was a different Sally, and her hopelessness was beginning to affect Joan. It wasn't only about staying safe, but also staying sane. She lived alone now, and that in itself was strange. She hadn't really adjusted to that, even though it had been some time now since Sally's father had died. The lockdown was getting to her. There was nothing she could do about it, and that made her unhappy too. To have no say in your life, in what you did, where you went, or who you saw... it was very undermining.

Chapter 8

Seb was aware he was in hospital, but he felt as if he were drifting. Drifting away from his body, away from everyone and everything. He wasn't sure whether he was dreaming or dying. It was strange, like being in a cloud up in the sky, and reality was fading. Images floated into his mind. His parents and sisters, his grandparents, his horses. Sally. A little boy with curly hair and blue eyes. Who was he? His son!

That's right, he thought. *Sally's expecting.* He had to get better. Had to see his son for real. Had to fight his way out of this cloying cloud and see his one and only, his beloved Sally.

Three weeks passed. Brianna rang the hospital every day, as did Sally. Both were beside themselves. Brianna and Marj were starting to feel better, and they put the horses back into their stables, just letting them out in the indoor school for exercise. Brianna was in constant touch with her parents. Marj's contact with her father and mother was more intermittent, as she wasn't that close to them. Their families had worried, but the two women had got through the virus with comparative ease.

After a few days, they felt well enough to exercise the horses properly and took them out for a hack. Brianna was riding and leading, as was Marj, so all the horses had work. When they returned to the yard, there was a strange horsebox waiting for them. A very dishevelled blonde woman got out of the cab. Without preamble, she said, 'I'm looking for Charlie Proctor.

Is he around?'

'He's in hospital,' Marj said shortly. She didn't much like the look of the woman and couldn't imagine what she wanted, especially as she was out and about during lockdown.

'Oh.' The woman looked nonplussed for a moment, then said, 'I've brought Goblin back. I'm giving him to Mr Proctor.'

Now it was Marj and Brianna's turn to stare.

'What do you mean?' Marj asked.

'What I said,' the woman snapped.

'But he's a valuable horse. Surely you don't mean give. You'll want money, and neither of us are in a position to negotiate with you.'

Much to their consternation, the woman burst into tears. Marj got down from her horse, as did Brianna.

'Let's put these away, then I think a cup of tea is in order,' Marj said.

Twenty minutes later, they led the still very upset woman upstairs.

'I'm guessing you're Clifford's partner,' Marj said gently, as Brianna made their drinks.

The woman nodded and swallowed hard. 'Yes, his wife. My name's Margaret. He's dead!'

Marj sucked in a breath. 'Oh, God. I'm sorry.'

'So am I!' Brianna came across and hugged the woman, who drew back. She gave Brianna a wan smile.

'You shouldn't do that. Social distancing, remember?'

'Sorry, I wasn't thinking. We've had Covid – what about you?'

'Cliff had it when he came to collect Goblin, but he wouldn't believe it. He died a couple of days later. I haven't been able to hold a proper funeral or anything. He's left such a muddle...

I don't know where to start. But I can't cope with Goblin. We have six other horses, and our groom quit just after Cliff died. I don't know much about looking after them. It was Cliff's thing, not mine. Oh, I used to help crew for him when he was doing a big ride, but really, I was just in the background. Cliff did say he was amazed by the difference in Goblin and that Charlie deserved more money than he'd charged.'

Brianna and Marj exchanged a look. Margaret saw it and gave another weak smile.

'I bet he disputed the bill. It was his way – he always did it, and sometimes, he'd get away with it. It was all bravado, really.'

'And you do know Goblin's a valuable horse?' Marj asked.

'Yes, I know what he's worth, but he's a constant reminder of Cliff. When Cliff got back from here, he collapsed, and he died a couple days later. All he talked about in between gulps for air was that fucking horse!' Margaret began sobbing again. 'It wasn't just Covid. He had a heart attack brought on by the virus.'

'We'll take Goblin, of course we will,' Marj said. 'The boss can sort it with you when he recovers. Now, Bri, where's that drink?'

While they drank their tea, Marj disappeared into her room. Brianna watched her go, wondering what she was up to.

Brianna found it hard to keep the conversation going. Margaret didn't have much more to say, so Brianna told her about her home and how her father wanted her to go into the family wine business. Just as she was running out of conversation topics, Marj emerged.

'Sorry about that, but I've been making a few phone calls.' She handed Margaret a piece of paper. 'If the first one on here can't help with your horses, the second will. But try the first to start with, as he has more experience.'

Margaret looked up at her with teary eyes. 'Thank you so much.'

Later, Brianna and Marj stood looking over the stable door at Goblin, who was tucking into his hay. He turned his head towards them, blowing gently through his nose, as if to say thank you.

'How do you think the boss will react?' Brianna asked Marj.

'I think he'll be pleased that Goblin's back. And that horse was so happy to see you, wasn't he?'

Brianna nodded. She'd been happy to see Goblin too. The pair of them had built a relationship before Clifford had picked him up, helped by Seb, who'd shown Brianna his methods and had her train Goblin under his supervision.

There'd been no change in Seb's condition, as Brianna found out when she rang the hospital. Hearing of Clifford's death had spooked her and Marj, and made them worry even more about their boss.

Sally was really struggling. She couldn't concentrate on her work and felt isolated and alone, though she spoke to her friends over the phone as often as she could. One of them did her shopping for her and left it at her door. She was terrified to go to the supermarket, worried about catching the virus and the effect it'd have on her unborn child.

The days dragged on and on. When Sally's boss rang her, she immediately burst into tears and unloaded on him, telling him even more than she had Joan. She knew her mother was concerned about her and didn't want to make it worse. So, she found herself telling him how she was feeling – worried Seb would die, worried he wouldn't come back to Australia if he lived, worried about her baby, worried about her family. Finding it hard to sleep, finding it hard to eat. Her list of troubles went on and on.

Ken, her boss, was very surprised. He'd always thought Sally was one of the most positive people he knew.

'It just goes to show,' he said later to his wife, 'you never know how people are really feeling.'

He'd agreed that the best thing for Sally to do was to go and live with her mother in Queensland, which was what Sally wanted in any case.

'Get everything in place,' he'd said, 'so when the border reopens, you'll be ready to roll.'

'And supposing it doesn't?'

'Doesn't what?'

'Reopen.'

'My dear girl, it will at some point. We're one country – the states can't be shut off from each other forever. The economy will drive them to reopen, and there's tourism to consider. Queensland relies on us Southerners going there to escape the winter blues.'

The next day, it was announced that the borders would reopen the month after. Sally felt better immediately and readied herself to leave. In the meantime, news also came through from England that Seb had turned a corner. At last, he was on the mend, though still very weak and tired. It was the boost Sally had needed to lift her spirits.

A week later, Brianna was again at the hospital to pick Seb up. An orderly brought him out in a wheelchair. She was horrified by his appearance – he'd lost weight, becoming pale and gaunt, and even his hair looked thin. He gave Brianna a weak smile as the orderly helped him into the car. It was plain he was still quite unwell, but the hospital was near breaking point and desperate for his bed.

Brianna drove home slowly. She chatted away, but didn't mention Goblin, as she thought it could wait. Seb didn't say much. His head was throbbing from the effort of getting to the car, and talking too much still made him cough.

The hospital had warned Brianna that he'd need care when he was home, and she and Marj had talked it through. Marj was more experienced with the horses, so she'd make that her main role, while Brianna looked after Seb. At that stage, though, they hadn't known how bad he'd be.

When they got back, Marj met them at the door. Seb announced he was going straight to bed.

'I guessed you would,' Marj said, 'so I've readied the bed. Bri and I will make you a drink and bring it up in a minute.'

Seb nodded. Part of his brain was telling him to stop being pathetic, but he was so tired. His legs were like jelly.

The two women watched him climb the stairs. He looked like he was thirty years older. It seemed inconceivable that a short time ago, he'd been an energetic, vibrant man. Now, he was a shadow of his former self.

When they took his coffee up, he was in bed with his eyes closed. Thinking he was asleep, they turned to go.

'I'm awake,' he said, faintly. 'That coffee smells good.'

They stepped back into the room.

'Now, tell me all that's been going on. How have you coped?'

'Well, the strangest thing happened,' Marj said, then looked at Brianna.

'What? Come on, you two. What?' For a moment, Seb sounded more like his old self.

'Goblin's here,' Brianna said. 'Clifford's wife brought him back. He—'

'Why? I've done all I can with him, and—'

'Let Bri tell you, Boss. It's not what you think.'

Brianna took a deep breath. 'Margaret turned up out of the blue with Goblin. Soon after Clifford came here, he went down with the virus. He passed away. I expect that's where you got it from. Margaret said she couldn't cope with looking at Goblin day in and day out. In fact, she's not coping at all, really, so she's gifted him to you. She doesn't want a bar of him. He reminds her of Clifford all the time. She brought his passport and everything with her and has put you down as his owner. It's all there.'

Seb pushed himself upright. 'Jesus, he's worth a lot of money, that horse. Does she know that?'

'Yes, she knows,' Marj said. 'They have several valuable horses, I think. Or rather, Clifford did. I don't think Margaret is really that interested in horses. Or maybe she was, because of him. I sorted her out some help – I know a few people who've lost their jobs because of Covid. I expect she'll sell as soon as she can.'

They talked a bit longer, until Marj noticed Seb's eyes were drooping and nudged Brianna. Seb was asleep before they'd left the room.

Chapter 9

A few weeks later, Sally's friend Chris shouted her dinner. Although pleased to see him, Sally felt uncomfortable being out, given all the Covid restrictions. Chris told her some of her fear likely stemmed from her pregnancy and isolation from loved ones. He was interested in hearing as much as she'd tell him about Seb and even more interested when she revealed they'd met when he ran away from home. Sally could've kicked herself, because Chris then started asking questions she wasn't prepared to answer. She became very evasive and unknowingly heightened his curiosity further.

She turned the conversation away from the topic, and Chris seemed to accept it.

'So, you're off to live with your mother,' he said. 'Where is she, exactly?'

'On the Sunshine Coast, near Maleny. I can't wait to see her.'

'Seb's parents live in Queensland too, don't they?'

'Yes, near a little town called Boonah, south-west of Brisbane.'

Again, his line of questioning put Sally on guard. He soon changed the subject, however, and she relaxed. But he had a motive Sally would never have guessed.

Near the end of their meal, he again asked about Seb.

'When do you think your boyfriend will be back? Will you visit his parents in the meantime?'

'Maybe. I'm not sure.'

'I have a mate up there who might know them. What's the surname again?'

Sally squirmed mentally. This was a Chris she hadn't seen before. Why all the questions? And she didn't think she'd ever told him Seb's surname. But then again, was she just being oversensitive? Chris was a mate, and she knew he cared about her.

'I didn't say,' she said. 'Sorry, Chris. I'm tired.'

'Ah, I'm asking too many questions. I still care about you, Sally. You know that, don't you?'

'Yes, yes, I do, but I still have a lot of packing to finish. Do you mind if we go now?'

A week later, the borders opened. As she drove out of Sydney, Sally thought about the conversation she'd had with Chris. Why had it unsettled her? Chris was probably just being overprotective... and maybe a little jealous.

She smiled to herself. *Surely not*, she thought, *but it's good for a girl's ego.*

She took the inland route to Queensland, and stopped off in Tamworth, visiting friends and family. Her uncle had employed Seb for a couple of weeks when he'd passed through ten years ago. He was delighted by Sally's news and said he'd come to the wedding if he was able. She also stopped in Glenn Innes, where she stayed the night, again visiting people she knew. She was pressed to stay longer, but wanted to get over the border as soon as possible, in case it slammed shut again.

Memories of meeting Seb surfaced. She'd loved him right from the very first time she saw him, when he'd been bedraggled, stressed and so unhappy. Very different to how he was now. But she also knew he could slip back into that sad person very easily. How was he really? Was he coping with the restrictions? She'd frightened herself with her feelings – how was he doing?

Her thoughts followed her like black shadows all the way into Queensland. She stopped again in Warwick for the night, as she'd found crossing the border very stressful, though she couldn't say why. She hadn't had any trouble. All her paperwork had been in place; she'd sailed through without a hitch. But she'd worried about it so much, and the baby, whom she'd felt moving for some time, had gone into overdrive. It was all exhausting. However, it was a mental exhaustion, not a physical one.

'Listen here, you,' she said to her tummy, 'just calm down. We'll ring Daddy soon and see how he is.'

Settling into her small hotel, she called Seb. Although he'd been home for some time, he was still struggling. The main worry was that he remained completely drained of energy – his legs felt as if they belonged to someone else.

'How are you, Seb? How is everything? I'm well on my way north, now.'

'I've told Brianna to go home as soon as she's able, and I'm giving her Goblin. He was gifted to me, so now I'm passing him on. He loves her. Besides, she'll treat him well, and it's a good compensation for her not being able to work the year with me. It's one way of paying Pierre, too, though he said he wasn't worried about the money. He just wants Bri back safe and sound.'

'What else do you think Pierre will say? He wanted to get horses out of her system.'

'I think that'd be very difficult. Remember what happened with my mum? She avoided horses for twenty years, but her love for them was always there, under the surface. Now, she rides every day, and she's so much happier. She said she hadn't realised how much she missed riding until she had the chance to do it again.'

'Do you want our baby to ride?'

'Of course. Are you sure you're okay? You aren't overdoing it, or anything?'

'I'm fine. Tomorrow, I'm calling in to see your parents on my way to Mum's.'

They chatted for a while, until Sally became too tired and had to say goodnight.

***

The next morning, a tall, grey-haired man cursed as he watched Sally drive away. He'd got a flat tyre. Now, he'd have to find his own way, as it'd be impossible to catch up with her.

It's funny, he mused. *She hasn't noticed she's been followed all the way from Tamworth. Too focused on other things, probably.*

Finally, having changed the tyre himself, he got into his car and set off once more. As he passed the turn-off to Toowoomba, he saw a car in the distance with its hazards going. Getting closer, he could see it was Sally. So far, no-one had stopped to help her.

He drove a little way past, did a U-turn, and came back. Sally was sitting in her car, looking worried. She started when he approached her window.

'Do you need help?' he asked.

Sally let her window down a fraction. 'No, I'm good, thanks. I've just called the RACQ.'

'What's the problem? I might be able to save you the wait.'

'No, really, it's okay. They said they'd be here soon.'

'If you're sure.'

He turned and walked back to his car. He'd been surprised by how lovely Sally had looked up close. A beautiful woman, indeed.

Sally watched him go with a slight frown on her face. He'd looked familiar, somehow, but she knew she'd never seen him before. It puzzled her.

Before long, a friendly man from the RACQ turned up and identified the problem. It was only a sensor issue, so Sally could drive on without a worry. He told her to get it fixed when she reached her mother's place.

Forty-five minutes later, Sally pulled into the Proctors' driveway. Almost before she'd left the car, Connie was hugging her tight. Sally laughed as they parted. 'Social distancing?'

'Oh, Lord, I'm sorry.' Connie looked mortified.

Sally smiled. 'We're nearly family, Connie. I was teasing.'

Then Alec appeared, and Sally was hugged all over again. While Connie hadn't changed much in the ten years since Sally had last seen her – she had a few more crow's-feet around her eyes, but that was all – Alec had aged quite a lot. He'd lost most of his hair and become rather stooped. He wore glasses, too, which he hadn't before.

'Sally, you look a million dollars,' he said. 'Being pregnant suits you!'

'Thank you. I feel much better now I'm out of isolation and on my way to see Mum. I just wish Seb could come home... I'm so worried about him.'

'We all are,' Connie said, 'but hopefully he'll get back soon. We'll cross our fingers.'

Connie had prepared a light lunch, and Sally found she was very hungry. Recently, her worry had suppressed her appetite. Today, however, in the company of Connie and Alec, she was starving. They regaled her with stories of Seb from when he was small and speculated whether his baby would also be a cheeky rascal.

'Do you know if it's a boy or girl?' Alec asked.

'No,' Sally said. 'We felt it's a bit like unwrapping a Christmas present early. I asked Seb, as I knew they'd check when I had the scan. He didn't want to know and nor did I. Most people do, it seems. They were surprised in the hospital, but all we want is for him or her to be healthy.'

Connie took her hand. 'We'd love it if you and your mum came and stayed with us. Eve and Joe – Alec's parents – left South Australia to come home but are now stuck in Victoria. It seems so strange. We're in the same country, but we still can't get together.'

Eventually, Sally reluctantly set off once more, as she still had a long journey ahead of her. As she drove past a disused driveway, she didn't notice the car partially concealed within it.

Chapter 10

Time passed both quickly and slowly. It seemed to take forever for Brianna to be cleared to go home, and for Goblin's transport to be arranged, but the time to leave was upon her before she could blink. Both Marj and Seb were sorry to see them go, but knew it was for the best. Pierre wasn't as put out as Seb had feared; he was just pleased to be getting his daughter home in the middle of a pandemic. When they waved Brianna off, she cried, and it made Seb and Marj feel emotional too. She'd looked after Seb well.

Seb was in a dilemma. He had a large property, three horses, and Marj to think of. He really didn't know what to do. In his original plan, Marj would've easily found a job, or chosen to relocate to Australia with him. She was very experienced with horses and had been with him almost since the moment he'd arrived in England. She was older than him, in her forties, and had devoted her life to horses. Although she'd had the occasional boyfriend, they'd never seemed to last long. Seb guessed horses were her first and last love.

He returned to his office, wondering what was best to do. Who was going to buy his place in the middle of a crisis? How was he going to get back home? It was dire in England, and he'd just heard there'd been a big spike of cases in Victoria, so they were in lockdown again. For how long, no-one knew.

He wasn't coping well. All his old demons were returning,

and he wanted to withdraw from the world and just be with his horses. Sally was so far away, and in some ways, his short time with her seemed more like a dream than reality. And a baby! What was he thinking? With his blood in its veins, what chance did it have of being a good person?

Shutting the door to his office, he started to go through his papers. He'd need to get everything organised if he was to sell and return to Australia, but he didn't get far. Suddenly, he felt so overwhelmed he just put his head in his hands and gave way to all his fears. Tears came, bitter tears, for his youth stolen by his monster of a grandfather. He hadn't revisited all that in many years; now, it all came flooding back. For a time, the black dog sat on his shoulder and refused to move.

At last, he pulled himself together and went in search of Marj. He found her in the tack room, polishing a saddle as if her life depended on it, and was horrified to see tears streaming down her face. He'd never seen Marj cry, even when her favourite horse, Zulu, had died of colic. It'd been a horrible end, but she'd been stoic, although sad.

'Marj, whatever is the matter?'

Seb put his arm around her shoulders. He'd never normally do anything like that, either. It was a day for strange, out-of-character happenings.

'I just got a message… my brother's died – that ghastly virus is to blame,' Marj said, wiping her tears.

'I didn't know you had a brother.'

'No, you wouldn't have. We fell out years ago and haven't spoken since. I always thought we'd make up one day, but now it's too late.'

'You poor girl.' Seb pulled her closer, until her head was resting against his chest. He knew only too well what it meant to have regrets – God, he had a few. With his free hand, he fished a rather grubby hankie out of his pocket and offered it to her. But Marj ignored it. The floodgates were well and truly open, and she seemed unable to stop sobbing. Seb thought it best to let her.

Eventually, she regained control of herself and sat upright again. She looked a real mess.

'Come on,' Seb said. 'Come over to the house, and we'll have a cup of coffee, or something. You look like you could do with a drink.'

He guided her across the yard, one hand at the small of her back. She was still distressed; he could feel her trembling as they made their way inside.

In the kitchen, Seb told her to sit while he went in search of alcohol. He came back with an unopened bottle of expensive French brandy, which he'd been gifted on that last trip to Bergerac, when he'd reconnected with Sally. He rarely drank and hadn't had any occasion to open it until now. He poured quite a generous portion into one of the brandy glasses he'd brought with him and a smaller measure for himself.

'So, what happened between you and your brother?' he asked, gently.

She sniffed and took a large gulp of brandy. It caught her throat and made her cough. Looking down into her glass, she said, 'My brother, Brian, is – was – younger than me and very clever. My parents thought he was destined for great things. Dad wanted me to go to university too, because he thought I should have a good career, but I refused. All I ever wanted to do was work with horses.'

Sniffing again, she scrubbed at her cheeks.

'I got accepted into the police force, with the goal of joining the mounted section. Mum and Dad backed me up, after some hesitation, though they didn't know I wanted to join the mounted section. Brian did. I don't really know why Dad was so deadset against horses, but when Brian let out the real reason I'd joined, he was furious. We rowed, but he couldn't do much about it. I'd joined the force, and that was that.'

Marj shook her head.

'Brian really turned against me. Looking back, I suppose he was jealous. He always said I got away with things he couldn't, which was silly. Dad and Mum treated us as equally as they could. Mostly, I took his sniping, but one day…'

She took another sip of brandy, then sighed.

'We were both at home. We hadn't seen much of each other for several months. Brian started spouting nasty things, saying I wasn't clever enough to go to uni and was horse-mad because I had a face that looked like a horse. I lost it, which was a surprise to both of us.'

She pressed her hands into her eyes.

'I hit him. We ended up fighting – literally. I pushed him, hard. He lost his footing and hit his head. Mum and Dad had been out and came back to find me trying to revive him. They called an ambulance, and he was taken to hospital. I was a probationary police officer. When Brian made an official complaint against me, my career ended before it had even started. It strained my relationship with my parents too.'

She drew in a shuddering breath. 'I'm sorry, Boss. I can't remember the last time I actually cried!'

'It's better to let these things out. Bottling them up helps no-one, least of all you.'

They sat in silence for a while, each busy with their own thoughts. Then, Marj said, 'I rather think you've had your share of troubles too.'

Seb looked down. He didn't want to relive the past, though lately, it'd seemed determined to haunt him again.

'When I was twenty, I did a very stupid thing and ran away from home, thinking the worst of a conversation I'd overheard. I'll always regret not waiting to find out the real story. The only good thing was that I met Sally and found some truths, at a terrible cost to myself.'

Abruptly, he stopped speaking. Marj waited, hoping to learn more. She had a huge amount of respect for her boss. His connection to horses was legendary, and he fascinated her. In some ways, his lifestyle was almost puritan; he didn't really drink or socialise, yet he could make even the stroppiest horse obedient within a very short time. Sometimes, Marj had felt he talked to horses more than humans. He'd always seemed immune to the opposite sex – though clearly, that wasn't the case, as recent events had shown.

'Your family are in Queensland, aren't they?' she said. 'Is that where your girlfriend lives?'

'She's moving up there now to be near her mother. Her father passed away a while ago.'

'How did you meet?'

Seb shrugged. 'Just by chance. We split up ten years ago, because I felt I wasn't good for her. I thought she'd find someone better, but...' He trailed off. 'I feel so blessed to have found her again. I love her to bits.'

As soon as the words left him, he was filled with embarrassment. What was he thinking, speaking like that? He looked down to find his glass empty. It wasn't good to drink on an empty stomach.

Marj got to her feet and came round the table, rather unsteadily. She, too, was feeling the effects of the brandy. Leaning down, she kissed his cheek. Not a peck, but a lingering kiss. Seb jumped up, almost knocking her over.

'Oh, God. Boss, I'm sorry.'

Seb recovered quickly. 'I think we both need some food inside us, don't you? I'll scramble some eggs. Sit down. No, better still – get some cutlery out while I cook. It's in that drawer.'

Seb pointed the drawer out, and Marj grinned suddenly.

'I do know where most things are in here,' she said. 'When you were laid up, I helped Bri cook a few times.'

'Ah, I'd forgotten.'

Later, when they'd eaten and cleared their dishes away, Marj turned to Seb. 'Thanks for everything. I'm sorry about… about, you know, kissing you. It won't happen again, I promise. I—'

Seb held up his hand to stop her.

'It's okay, Marj. We're living a strange life at the moment. Nothing is normal. In fact, I was just thinking – why don't we share our meals for the time being? At least until you've found another job. It'd be silly, really, for you to eat alone across the yard, while I'm eating alone here. What do you say?'

Marj thought it was a brilliant idea, as she hated cooking but liked eating, so it was arranged. She soon found out Seb was a good cook, and his delicious food made her feel far more positive about her future.

Later, lying in bed, Marj thought over the day's events and realised she had deep feelings for her boss.

God, that won't do, she thought, as she drifted off to sleep.

Chapter 11

When Seb told Sally that he and Marj were sharing the cooking, she felt a strong stab of jealousy. Then Seb let slip that Marj had kissed him on the cheek. Of course, Sally had never met Marj, and her imagination played tricks on her, making her feel even worse. She was cross with herself, as she knew it was foolish, but she wanted to be with Seb so badly that it was almost consuming her. Again, she was hovering on the cusp of depression.

'What's the matter with me, Mum?' she asked, curled up on Joan's coach with her head on her mother's lap. 'I know I'm being silly, but it doesn't help. I just want Seb here with me.'

'Sweetheart, you're pregnant, and the world is in turmoil. Of course you want Seb here beside you. It's natural to feel jealous of this groom; she has time with him that you don't. Still, I'm sure he's faithful to you. You told me he'd been with no-one else in the ten years you were apart. He's not going to start looking elsewhere now, is he?'

Connie was also worrying about her son. She knew he was having trouble selling up and getting home. With her parents-in-law stuck in Victoria, she sometimes wondered if the family would ever get back together. Her sister Carmel was also in Victoria, but they'd drifted apart again, and Connie wasn't sure where she was exactly. As Queensland began to return to normal – a new normal, but at least their business was running again – Connie's thoughts increasingly turned to her son and her sister. She hadn't heard from Carmel since a card at Christmas, which hadn't had a forwarding address, and she knew Carmel had moved on since. To where, though, she had no idea. They'd never been close, but she wished she'd made more of an effort to stay in touch.

The Proctors' business was back up. Although they were in a drought, there was always farm machinery that wanted mending, so Alec did more and more of that sort of work. At the beginning of August, an older man brought in a large ride-on mower to be repaired. It seemed the man, who said his name was Don, had left it at the top of a steep bank, and the whole thing had slithered down and ended up in a scrambled mess at the bottom. Don explained he was employed by the mower's owner, who was away, and thought he may get the sack if he didn't get it mended himself.

'You've done a good job here, mate,' said Alec. 'It'll take a while to fix, and it'll be expensive, I'm afraid.'

'Can't be helped,' Don replied, as he stood watching Alec examine it. He was tall and thin, with a wispy beard and his hat pulled down low.

'Give it a week, and I'll ring you,' Alec said.

'Lost my mobile, haven't I? Don't worry, I'll just come back. Nice set-up you have here. Got many working for you?'

Alec was uncomfortable. There was something odd about this bloke; his eyes were everywhere. Was he casing the place?

'What's your boss's name, then?' Alec asked. 'I need it for the invoice.'

'Make it out to me. I'll have to pay in any case.'

Alec scratched his head. 'I'd know your boss for sure. It won't be a problem, as far as I can see.'

'Just address it to Don. Don Glover. Best be off, I've got things to do. See ya.'

The man got into his ute and was gone almost before Alec drew breath. Alec watched him go, frowning. There'd been something vaguely familiar about him, though what, Alec wasn't sure. His behaviour was strange too. Why was he reluctant to say where he worked? And why hadn't Alec seen him around before? He knew most people in the area – if not their names, then at least where they fitted in.

Alec took another look at the mower. It was quite old, and that was odd. The places where it was bent and buckled were going rusty. It was plain the so-called accident hadn't happened recently. Alec kicked himself. He'd been so busy studying the stranger that he hadn't looked at the mower very closely. Who did the man remind him of? He wished he could remember.

A few minutes later, Connie walked down from the house. 'You'll never believe this, but Carmel's been in touch,' she said. 'She was drifting from job to job, but Covid's trapped her in Wangaratta. She was working in a saddlery business, which of course is shut now. She's on benefits and going nuts being stuck at home, so she rang for a chat… she was jealous when I told her we're pretty much normal here. Alec, I don't think you heard a word I said!'

'I had this strange bloke in. He brought a mower, saying it'd just been damaged, but it looks old to me. The damage, I mean. He kept looking round – more up towards the house than anywhere else, now I think about it.'

Connie gave an involuntary shiver. 'I hope he isn't planning on stealing anything.'

'So long as he doesn't steal you, love.'

'Don't be daft! Who'd steal me?'

'I would, for starters. Seriously, though, we'd better keep an eye out. He worried me.'

When Connie returned to the house, she didn't see the figure watching her from the bushes near the road. The man nodded to himself, then walked back to the ute he'd parked some distance away. All he needed was courage and the right opportunity.

***

In England, Seb finally got buyers for his horses. They didn't pay as much as he would've received normally, but it was a fair price, and they had good homes – he'd made sure of that. Marj was desperately looking for another job, but so far without luck. She seemed to have got over the worst of her grief about her brother and had talked to her mother on the phone a few times, though Seb got the impression they hadn't been very happy conversations.

Getting a flight back to Australia was proving difficult, and Seb really wanted to sell his property first. He was on the phone nearly every day, trying to get an agent interested. Because it was essentially a horse establishment, the market was more limited, and a few agents refused to accept it in the current climate.

His depression was taking a deeper hold. The black dog seemed his constant companion, always lurking like some medieval beast waiting to grab him. At least Marj was with him, and they had dinner together most nights, where he had to make an effort to be more upbeat.

They'd fallen into a routine. Seb would cook, while Marj laid the table and cleared up afterwards. Occasionally, they'd share some wine, though they both drank very little. After her episode with the brandy, Marj didn't really trust herself. She was very aware of how kind and lovely Seb was, and he was so good-looking. She'd realised with horror that she'd fallen in love with him. It was the first time in her life she'd felt this way about a man, any man, and it made her uncomfortable. Eventually, she became so aware of his presence that she started to avoid him, making excuses not to eat with him.

Seb couldn't understand what was going on. Marj seemed to be blowing hot and cold. One minute, she couldn't do enough for him. The next, she was unfriendly and distant. Then he found a buyer, or rather his agent did. The process was entirely digital, as the buyer was from the Middle East and didn't want to risk flying into England, even though its borders weren't shut. He'd been looking to buy in the area for some time, as he wanted to start up an Arab horse stud. He was prepared to pay an amount beyond Seb's wildest dreams: enough that Seb would be able to pay off the mortgage and have quite a large nest egg left over. He accepted quickly, before the buyer could change his mind, and agreed to stay on as caretaker until he got a flight back to Australia. At last, things seemed to be falling into place.

Marj was very unhappy. Now she'd admitted to herself how she felt about Seb, she was even more upset that he'd sold up and would soon be gone. If he had his way, at least. Part of her knew it was inevitable, but another hoped it wouldn't happen, and by some miracle, he'd stay in England.

It seemed fate was on her side. There were hardly any flights going to Australia, and most of them had been booked months ahead. One good thing was that Seb could now afford a flight, as the price had gone up and up. He'd been unable to book before because he hadn't wanted to leave until he had everything neat and tidy in England.

It was now August, and six months since Seb had seen Sally. A few doubts were creeping in. He'd reacted instinctively – both of them had. He'd always loved her, but did she truly love him? Of course she did, she was carrying his child. But had she tricked him into marriage? Of course not. She'd been upset when she'd told him she was pregnant, even offering to have an abortion if he didn't want the child. What had he been thinking? A *child!* It might grow up to have its great-grandfather's rotten genes. The negative thoughts swirled round and round in his head.

Marj wasn't coping very well either. She'd always been a busy person, so was now finding it hard to occupy herself. Seb had put the saddles, bridles and harnesses up for sale, and that'd kept her attention for a time, while people came and looked. However, as they were all in immaculate condition, and Seb had been nearly giving them away, that episode hadn't lasted long. He'd also sold some of the furniture in the main house. The furniture in the flat the girls had used was staying put, so Marj didn't have to worry about that. Now she wasn't keen on going to the main house, as it was almost an empty shell. Some nights, she went across to have dinner, and some nights she didn't, as this also played a factor in her behaviour.

One hot afternoon, she was trawling through the Horse & Hound looking for work when Seb poked his head through the door.

'Are you coming across for dinner tonight, Marj? I have some beautiful fillet steaks. Didn't realise they were in the freezer, or they would've gone long ago.'

Marj kept her head down, as sudden tears threatened. Why, she didn't know. She shook her head vigorously. 'Thanks, but no, not tonight. I have an advertisement to answer, and a few phone calls to make. I...' She trailed off, not knowing what other excuse to give.

Seb stood in the doorway with a puzzled expression on his face. 'Have I done something? You seem to be hiding away, these days.'

'No!' Marj's voice was loud enough to shock her. Seb took a step back.

'Okay, okay. I was just asking.'

With that, he turned and left. Marj opened her mouth to call after him, but no sound came out.

While Seb walked back across the yard, he noticed there were a few weeds springing up. I'll have to deal with them, he thought, though he was still puzzled over Marj's strange behaviour. He decided to leave the steaks. Maybe she'd want them tomorrow. He had quite a lot of eggs, as they had a few chickens – something he'd been grateful for during this odd year. In the end, he made a frittata, as he had quite a lot of veggies too and he enjoyed cooking. Later, he rang Sally. As usual, their conversation was a rollercoaster of emotion.

'I'm on a waiting list to get a flight home, Sal,' he said. 'That's all I can tell you. The number of cases is climbing again here – it's shocking. Thank goodness I live in the country, not in a town or city. At least that's something to be grateful for.'

'Bugger that, I just want you home! I don't feel grateful for anything right now. I'm getting big... soon, I'll be waddling, and you won't love me anymore. Maybe you don't now, and not getting a flight is just an excuse.'

'Oh, you know that's not true. Don't cry, darling, please. I can't hug you from here. Please don't cry, or I will too.'

They'd had several similar conversations before. Neither of them was coping very well with the situation, partially because they'd only found each other so recently.

After Seb had finally finished talking to Sally, he looked at the clock. It was earlier than usual, because Sally and her mother were driving down to see Seb's parents and wanted to get away in good time. He considered phoning his mum but wasn't really in the right frame of mind. Unusually for him, he poured a generous glass of whisky, then took it upstairs and got into bed. Sipping the whisky, he picked a book to read from the pile on his nightstand. However, the words were dancing across the pages. He put the book down, finished his whisky and let himself drift off to sleep.

Marj was cross with herself. Why had she turned down Seb's offer of dinner? It was no different to any other time. But it is, she told herself. I don't want to make a fool of myself again. She boiled an egg, feeling very sad and out of sorts. There were two bottles of wine in the cupboard, one red and one white, which Brianna had brought with her.

Why not? Marj thought. She opened the white. Rummaging in her belongings, she fished out a photo album she'd carted around for years but hadn't looked at. It was full of pictures of her parents and her brother and herself, from back when life had been simple, and she'd been happy. There she was, on holiday with her brother, making sandcastles. She sat for some time, looking at the photos. Some made her laugh. Some made her cry. She went to take another sip of wine and found she'd drunk the whole bottle. Hell, there was another bottle – red, but it didn't matter.

She got to her feet, rather unsteadily, then went into the kitchen and opened the other bottle. Pouring herself a glass, she swigged most of it down. What's the boss doing? she wondered. Maybe I should take the bottle across and share it with him.

It seemed to take her a long time to get down the stairs and out into the yard. No lights were on in the main house, but there was enough of a moon to illuminate her way. 'Hm,' she said. 'Looks like he's gone to bed.'

The back door wasn't locked, so she made her way indoors. Everything looked neat and tidy in the kitchen as far as she could see. I'll go wake him up, then we can share the wine, she thought.

She climbed the stairs. She'd helped Brianna when he was ill, so she knew where his room was. As she wobbled her way over to his bed, she could hear him breathing deeply.

'Boss,' she whispered. No response. She set the bottle down quietly on the bedside table. Pity to wake him. I'll just get into bed for a cuddle. I'm sure he won't mind. Her head was swimming. She managed to pull off her shorts and t-shirt, but her underwear was beyond her, as standing on one leg or holding onto the bedhead to stop herself from falling made undoing her bra difficult. Seb, having consumed the large whisky earlier, slept on, oblivious to what she was up to.

Giving up on her clothing, Marj slithered into bed. She put her arm over his chest and snuggled up to him. He turned towards her.

'Sal?' he murmured. Then his eyes flew open. Although it was dark, Marj could see them glittering. 'What the hell?'

Marj was too drunk to be fazed. 'Just thought we could have a cuddle. Sorry, didn't mean to frighten you.'

Seb leapt out of bed. After yanking on his pants, as he slept in the nude, he put on the bedside light. Marj covered her eyes, and he saw the bottle by the bed. 'How much wine have you had?'

'Nothin' much,' Marj said, with a giggle. 'Come back! All I want is a cuddle.'

'What you need is to get out of my bed and drink a strong coffee.'

Grumbling to herself, Marj struggled out of bed. Then, to Seb's horror, she started to fumble with her bra. Finally undoing it, she waved it in the air in triumph.

'How's that?' She danced across the room, bent over, and was violently sick. Most of it landed on a chair, with some splattering the floor.

Seb was frozen to the spot. He had no idea what to do. Marj sank down into a crouch and started to cry – loud, raw sobs. Seb found himself becoming angry, very angry, an emotion that he rarely gave in to.

'Get dressed, then clean up this mess. I'll see you downstairs.'

He grabbed his dressing gown and stomped out. Being sick and seeing Seb's anger had sobered Marj up considerably. She managed to put her bra and her t-shirt back on, though for a time, her shorts refused to cooperate. When she finally managed to get them on, they were back-to-front. Still crying quietly, Marj pulled them on the right way, then remembered her vomit. Going down to the laundry, she got a bucket and mop to clean it up. Fortunately, the floor in the bedroom wasn't carpeted, though the chair was upholstered. It took her a good half hour to get everything clean.

By the time she crept into the kitchen, Seb had calmed down. Hearing her coming, he started to pour her a coffee. 'Sit down,' he said.

Marj was shocked. He looked pale, drawn and ten years older. If she'd had a mirror, she would've been equally shocked by her own appearance. Her hair was wild, her face blotchy and tear-stained, her clothes crumpled, grubby and smeared with vomit.

He put a cup of coffee in front of her, then poured another for himself and sat down opposite her. 'Listen to me, Marj,' he said. 'This is hard for both of us, but getting drunk won't help anyone. I'm sure finding another job is hard under the present circumstances, but you'll find one soon. In fact, a bloke I know up in Scotland is looking for a groom. I was going to ring him tomorrow.'

Fresh tears flowed down Marj's face. 'I've blown that too, now, haven't I? I'm so sorry, Boss. I don't know what came over me. I'll pack my stuff up in the morning and be gone as soon as I can.'

Seb considered her for a few moments. 'Look, I don't want you to run off. I did that once, and running away doesn't solve anything. Go back to the flat, have a shower and a good sleep, and we'll talk again tomorrow. I'm not going to sack you. Okay?'

Marj gulped. She seemed to be making up for all the years she hadn't cried.

'Boss, I'll never do anything like that again, I promise. I—'

She stopped as Seb held up his hand.

'That's enough for tonight. In fact, it's nearly morning. Go and sleep; we'll talk later.'

Marj got to her feet. Slowly, she went out of the house and across the yard to her flat. She lay down on her bed without changing and went to sleep quite quickly.

Seb, however, found his room still stinking of vomit. Looking at the chair, he could see it was still in a bad state.

'Bugger you, Marj,' he said.

He took himself off to his spare room and collapsed down onto the old sofa. Tired though he was, sleep eluded him. His thoughts turned first to Sally, then to his family. God, how he wished he'd sold up as soon as he'd returned from France. If only he'd been able to see the future. But then, if that were possible, his whole life would've been very different.

He didn't get to sleep until the first fingers of light were stealing across the eastern sky. Then, when he did, nightmares of his grandfather invaded his dreams.

Chapter 12

Sally woke and stretched luxuriously. Sleeping in Seb's old bed seemed to have soothed her, even though it hadn't been used since he left for England. It was seldom anyone came to stay, and Connie tended to put them in other bedrooms if they did. Somehow, though, it was fitting for Sally to stay there. When she and Seb had spoken the night before, he'd sounded strange but had assured Sally he was just tired. Sally had been tired too, so for once, their conversation had been short.

Winter was nearly over. It was a beautiful bright morning, and Sally decided to go for a walk. She was trying to keep as fit as being pregnant allowed. Alec, who was sitting at the kitchen table reading a magazine, looked up as she entered.

'Hi, love, how're you going? Want a coffee or tea?'

'No, thanks. I'm going for a little walk. Does Pip want to come too?' She petted the old Labrador.

'He might, though he's got rather lazy lately. Old age, I reckon.'

'Come on, boy,' Sally coaxed.

Pip looked very unenthusiastic but got to his feet and followed her out of the house. They walked down the short drive, and turned left once they reached the road, towards the sunrise. Sally enjoyed the colours; the bushland lining the road seemed to have been drawn with a golden pen. Not far down, there was an area of bushland that was quite dense in places. It was so beautiful and peaceful.

Pip was lagging behind her, as he didn't like the gravel much. He was getting old, and usually, he didn't go far. His pads were more tender than they used to be. Sally heard him give a low growl, then a sharp bark. Turning, she saw him looking into the dense undergrowth, his hackles up. He looked like a ball of angry fluff.

'What's up, boy?' she said. As she approached him, his barking became more frenzied, until he was bouncing on the spot. Still, he didn't seem game to go up the little bank and into the undergrowth.

Sally peered in. There was movement – a figure melted into the bushes further back. It made the hair stand on the back of her neck.

'Who's there?' she called. 'What do you want?'

All was quiet, aside for the chattering of birds deep in the undergrowth. It was enough to make her turn back, and she covered the five hundred metres back to the driveway much faster than she had on her way out.

'That was quick,' Alec said, as she walked into the kitchen. 'You look worried. What's the matter?'

'Pip started barking at something – or some*one* – in the bushes down the road. It was spooky, as if someone was watching me.'

Alec was about to speak when Connie came in, closely followed by Joan.

'Something wrong?' asked Connie.

By now, Sally had begun to feel silly. Had it just been her imagination going into overdrive? It could've been anything, and the likelihood of it being a person was really rather low.

'I thought there was someone in the bushes down the road...

or rather, Pip did. I looked, and there was something. Just a roo, I expect.'

'There have been a few around lately,' Alec said. 'More than I've seen in a long time. We're back in drought again, which makes them bolder. Funny place for them, though. They usually prefer the paddocks to the bush.'

The three women drove off into Brisbane to do some baby shopping. As they came out of the driveway, turning right, they saw a tall man walking down the road to their left. He glanced behind him. He was too far away for them to see his face, but on spotting them, he visibly quickened his pace.

Bugger, the man thought. *I'm getting careless. I don't want to be found out yet!*

He hurried down the road a little further, then got in his car, which was still parked in the overgrown driveway. He sat for a time, going over his options. Eventually, he concluded it was far too early to act. He didn't know when Seb was returning from England, and it had given him a shock to see Sally pregnant. He'd just have to be patient and wait.

A coughing fit overtook him, and he fumbled for his inhaler. Time was getting short, but he intended to finish what he'd started.

***

Seb decided to go and talk to Marj. He'd only seen her briefly in the morning. She'd looked as bad as he felt, and they'd agreed to speak later, but then Seb's buyer had phoned him with a whole list of questions. He'd got stuck in paperwork, and now it was evening again. Having spoken briefly to Sally, he decided he'd have to confront Marj, though he wasn't really prepared for it.

He tapped on the door. There was no response. He tapped

again, feeling his heart rate shoot up. She hadn't done anything silly, had she? He was about to knock a third time when the door opened. Marj stood there, looking even worse than before, which Seb wouldn't have thought possible. They stared at each other, then Seb said, 'Can I come in?'

She moved aside without speaking. Everything was sparkling clean, and it was obvious how she'd spent her day. Without waiting to be asked, Seb sat down. Marj remained standing. Her flat might have been tidy, but she looked as if she'd been dragged through a hedge backwards.

'Sit down, Marj. You're making me nervous.'

This brought the glimmer of a smile to her face, and she sat.

'Last night never happened, as far as I'm concerned,' Seb said. 'I've just spoken to the bloke up in Scotland who I mentioned. He wants to interview you, and we've set up a Zoom meeting, tomorrow at nine o'clock sharp. How does that sound?'

'I don't know what to say, Boss. Looking back, yesterday seems like some awful nightmare. What was I thinking? Or rather, not thinking? I've never been drunk in my life, and I've certainly never behaved like that either. I don't remember much, to be honest.'

'What do you remember?'

'Coming across the yard, thinking we could share the wine. I'd already drunk a whole bottle. Then it's all very hazy, until I was sick and half-naked in your bedroom... oh, God, what did I do?'

'Nothing to worry about. You were a little amorous, but it's better if you don't remember.'

'I remember getting into your bed, and you were asleep, then furious.'

'Not sure if furious is the right word, but it doesn't matter. More importantly, are you up for this Zoom meeting tomorrow?'

'I am. Thank you, Boss.'

'Right. I'm going to turn in, so I'll see you in the morning.'

With that, Seb got to his feet and left. Marj stood at the window and watched him cross the yard. She wondered if Sally knew how lucky she was. Some would've taken advantage of Marj, and others would've sacked her on the spot. Seb was different. She knew then that she'd always love him; no-one would ever fill his shoes. She sighed. Pulling herself together, she made herself a sandwich, then showered and went to bed.

The next morning, she was a bundle of nerves. However, her interviewer was so laid-back that she soon forgot about being anxious.

'This is really only a formality, as Charlie is so well-known and respected that anyone who works for him will have good credentials,' he said. 'I gather you've been with him a long time?'

'Yes,' she said, and after answering a few more questions, the interviewer told her the job was hers.

A few minutes later, she found herself walking across the yard, feeling both surprised and excited. She knew it was time to leave. The boss was set to go back to Australia, and the others had long since left. It'd been a very strange time. Things might never be the same again, but for now, she was looking forward to a new job far away from here. She'd only ever been to Scotland once, as a child on a family holiday, and she'd been quite small, so she remembered little of it. It'd be good to start afresh.

Two days later, she managed to hold herself together when she said goodbye to Seb. If anything, he was the emotional one, as he pressed an envelope into her hand.

'Look after yourself, Marj,' he said. 'You're a great woman and wonderful with horses. You were a big part of the success story we had going here, and don't you ever forget it.'

He gave her a quick hug. She didn't open the envelope until

later, when she'd reached a service station. Inside was a photo of her on Zulu, a big warmblood they'd trained a while back. He'd been very difficult, but like Brianna with Goblin, Marj had formed a bond with him. He'd been special to her, and she'd been devastated when he died of colic. There she was, sitting on his back, looking pleased with herself. On the other side, Seb had written: 'To the best mate any horse or man could have. Best wishes, Charlie Proctor.'

Marj blinked tears away. It felt like Zulu had died so long ago, but it'd only happened last year. So much had changed... it seemed like another world.

***

Seb walked back to the house. It'd been strange before, but it was worse now, with everyone gone. He'd sold most of his furniture, and the house echoed. It was horrible. He entertained the idea of staying at the local pub, but quickly dismissed it. After all, he'd promised the new owners he'd take care of the place until they found someone else.

The rest of the day, he mooched about without doing anything very productive. Once again, the black dog was sitting on his shoulder. He was even finding it hard to cook. It all seemed a waste of time. He knew he had to eat, but the fridge was almost empty, and he didn't feel like shopping. In fact, he didn't feel like doing anything at all – just sitting and letting past regrets overshadow him.

When he got into bed, having watched a mindless programme on television that he couldn't remember anything about afterwards, he felt wide awake. However, Sally was out for the day with their mothers, so he couldn't speak to her until the morning. After tossing and turning most of the night, he finally fell asleep.

He was in a dark tunnel. Saul was behind him with a rifle. He was running, and though he could see the exit, he couldn't get any closer. Saul was catching up. Seb could feel his breath on the back of his neck.

'Grandson, are you? I'll make you pay.'

He got hold of Seb's collar, choking him.

Seb woke with a start, sweating and coughing, his heart rate through the roof. He scrambled out of bed and sat on the floor, putting his head in his hands.

'Oh, Sally, I wish you were here,' he muttered.

In the bathroom, he poured himself a glass of water. There was a packet of paracetamol in the cupboard. Maybe he should take the lot. He didn't know if he'd ever see Sally and his baby, and the Australian authorities weren't helping. He was one of their own, but he'd been abandoned because he lived abroad. Returning seemed impossible. And Sally would get over it. He wasn't any good for her, anyway. He'd told her that before.

He picked up the bottle and filled his glass with water.

**

Sally had a wonderful morning in the big Brisbane shopping centre, choosing baby things with Connie and Joan, from strollers to clothing to soft toys. Though she missed Seb, she refrained from saying so. At midday, they stopped for a coffee, idly watching people walk past while they chatted.

Suddenly, Connie gasped and clutched her cup, spilling some of her coffee down her front. She told Joan and Sally that she thought she'd seen someone who reminded her of her past. Although she said she was fine, she looked so pale and drawn that both other women insisted on ending their trip and going home.

That evening, Seb didn't join their usual video call. Sally tried and tried to reach him, and eventually, panic set in. Both Connie and Joan tried to reassure her, but Sally was beside herself.

'Is there anyone who lives near that might help, Connie?' Joan asked. 'Someone who could go and visit and see if he's okay? It's morning there, so perhaps he's just doing jobs and hasn't got his phone with him.'

'Come on, Sally,' Connie said. 'Getting so upset won't do the baby any good. I'm sure he's okay – call it a mother's intuition. I'd know if there was something wrong.' Connie patted her shoulder. 'We'll give it another five minutes, then try again. In the meantime, I'll put my thinking cap on as to who I could ring to go and check on him.'

Sally tried hard to pull herself together, but five minutes seemed like a lifetime. Then, her phone beeped. It was Seb. The moment Sally answered the call, she burst into tears. 'Oh, thank God. Where have you been? Didn't you have your phone with you? Are you alright?'

Seb gave a little chuckle. 'Whoa, slow down.'

'Seb, I was worried sick! We arranged when we would call, and it's a lot later than we said!'

'Darling, I'm sorry, I really am. I was feeling like shit last night, then I had a bad dream. When I woke, I admit I considered doing something very silly, though it was only a fleeting thought. When I looked outside, it was just getting light, and I remembered how I used to get up early and run. So, I did. I'm not as fit as I was, but it felt so good to be running again that I lost track of time. I passed a paddock full of cows and calves, and the sun came up in an orange glow, tinting their coats with gold... the dew on the grass looked like diamonds, and rooks and other birds were cawing and singing. It was all so English and beautiful that I realised I could cope after all. Why would I throw in the towel when surrounded by all this beauty? I have a wonderful woman waiting for me, and I'm going to be a dad. I feel so lucky.'

The three women sat with tears in their eyes after this little speech.

'Oh, Seb,' Sally said, 'I feel blessed to have you too. Thank goodness you went out for a run instead. Are you going to keep running after this?'

'Well, I don't have any horses to ride or train, so I guess so. I just hope I can get on a plane soon. Maybe I'll get lucky. I'm half expecting the guy who'll be in charge here to arrive and take over in any case.'

Joan and Connie discreetly left, to give them time to chat alone, but Sally gave an enormous yawn.

'Time for bed, I think,' said Seb.

'I wish you were with me.'

'So do I. After my run, I feel more positive than I have lately, so here's hoping.'

As Sally kept yawning, they reluctantly said goodnight.

After breakfast, Seb settled down to make sure all his paperwork was in order, so the changeover to the new owner would be as smooth as possible. *It's strange,* he thought. *I'm more optimistic than I have been for a long time. Has running made me feel this way?*

From then on, every morning, he got up early and went running. There were quite a few bridlepaths and green lanes around where he lived. The autumn mornings were very beautiful, as September was now well underway. The trees were turning orange, yellow and red, and some mornings, it was slightly frosty. The white grass seemed to make the brilliant colours of the changing leaves even more vivid. His new routine calmed and relaxed him, and he started to sleep better.

A week later, the new owner called to tell him he'd found a

manager to run the place, who'd be arriving with the first horses. Seb made sure the stables were shipshape and free of cobwebs. He organised fresh bedding and feed, then turned his attention to the house. He'd already sent his belongings to Australia via container, so all he had to do was pack his few clothes and personal effects, then settle down to wait. He'd booked himself accommodation at the local pub but was still hoping he'd get a flight out soon.

Three days later, he had an email from the owner, who said the manager had arrived with his family. Seb drove to the pub with his belongings, then returned to wait for the new arrivals. A big horse truck rolled in, closely followed by a top-of-the-range Merc. Then suddenly, it was people and horses everywhere. An extremely beautiful Arab stallion was first out of the truck. When he got to the bottom of the ramp, he paused, taking in his surroundings with interest. Seb, who'd watched the proceedings from afar, approached the horse, only for the groom holding him to put up a hand.

'Don't come near. He's a bit stressed.'

Seb stopped. 'It's okay, I won't worry him.'

The horse looked at Seb, then suddenly took a few steps over to him, almost pulling the lead rope out of the groom's grip. Seb held out his hand. After sniffing it, the horse put his head against Seb in a gesture of affection. The groom stood with his mouth hanging open.

'Jesus,' he said. 'I've never seen anything like it. I heard you were some kind of whisperer, but hell. What did you do?'

'Nothing.' Seb grinned. 'He just knows I like him. Do I detect an Aussie accent?'

'Yeah. Been over here for donkey's years, though.'

'Any thoughts of going back?'

'Nah, got nothing much to return for. You?'

'My girlfriend's over there, and I can't wait to get back,' Seb said, patting the horse's neck. 'Come on, let's get this chap into his new quarters. You've got others in the truck too?'

'Two older mares, and two younger. The young ones are a little flighty, so I'll let you handle them, if you don't mind.'

'Sure.' Seb was suddenly filled with happiness. He wasn't sure whether it was because the guy was Australian, or because he had another chance to work with horses, but he felt lighter than he had in some time.

'Wait.' A sharp voice rang out behind them. The stallion laid his ears back and snorted. 'I'm Giles Dean, the manager,' said the person striding up to them. 'What are you doing? This horse needs to be put in the stable right away. It can't be standing around here.' He looked at the man holding the rope. 'Are you the new groom?'

'Sure am. Name's Sid.'

Seb could hear an undertone of dislike in Sid's voice, though he doubted Giles would've picked it up.

'And you're Charles Proctor, previous owner of this place?'

'Yes.' Ever polite, Seb held out his hand. Giles ignored it.

'I'll take over now. Sid, follow me.'

Sid and Seb exchanged a glance, and Sid went to lead the stallion away.

'Come on, old chap,' he said. The horse looked a Seb with his huge brown eyes, then followed Giles and Sid into the stable block.

Seb stood still for a minute or two, unsure what to do. Then, he heard noises coming from inside the truck, so he walked up the ramp to have a look. The four mares were penned individually. As he studied them, a haughty voice said, 'Hey, you! What do you think you're doing? Come out. Those horses are very expensive, and we don't want them to be upset.'

A blonde woman was standing at the bottom of the ramp. Seb approached her, and held out his hand, wondering if she'd be as disagreeable as her partner. She wasn't; once she saw the tall, dark, handsome man in front of her, her manner changed considerably.

'Oh, I'm sorry. You must be Mr Proctor. My name is Faye – so pleased to meet you.'

'Yes, but call me Charlie.' As they shook hands, Seb was aware of her grey eyes assessing him closely. 'Do you want me to show you around the house?' he asked. 'First, though, I told Sid I'd help him with the mares.'

'Oh, I'm sure he'll be fine.'

Giles appeared, with Sid behind him, scowling. Seb went to join Sid, but Giles said, 'We can manage, thank you.'

'Right.' Seb stepped back.

The two men went up the ramp and came out leading the pair of older horses. They were fairly calm. Both stopped when they got to the bottom of the ramp, and one pulled towards Seb, but they allowed themselves to be led into the stable block. The two younger mares were getting restless and making a lot of fuss. Although Seb was tempted to go back up and calm them, he decided against it. It was plain Giles wasn't happy to see him and didn't want him near the horses, though Seb couldn't understand why.

Faye watched indecision flit across Seb's face. 'We heard you're an exceptional trainer. Is that right?' she asked.

Seb grinned at her. 'I do my best.'

'Giles was reading up about you. You have a lot of fans worldwide, it seems.'

Seb now understood Giles's hostility. 'Yes, well, it's exaggerated,' he said, uncomfortable. 'I'm just lucky that animals like me. Horses, especially.'

Faye smiled. 'I can understand that.' It was plain she liked the look of him, which made him feel even more uncomfortable.

There had been a lot of banging in the horsebox. A red-faced Giles and a calmer Sid appeared, leading the two young mares out. Both horses were sweating, and both men plainly had their hands full. As they reached the bottom of the ramp, one horse shot forward, yanking her rope out of Giles's hands, burning his palms. Seeing what had happened to her travelling companion, the other mare clearly thought to follow suit, but Sid was ready for her. He dug his heels in before she had the chance to escape. She leapt about, and it took all of Sid's skill to hang on. Meanwhile, the other horse careened across the yard and come to an abrupt halt by the back fence. Two other people appeared from the front of the truck – the driver and a spare groom. They started off in pursuit of the horse, who was clearly freaking out.

'Wait!' Seb called, with such authority that they all stopped and looked at him.

Giles scowled. 'We've got to catch her before she hurts herself.'

'Just wait a moment, and I'll get her.'

Looking even more belligerent, Giles folded his arms. 'This, I would like to see.'

Seb walked across the yard but stopped a couple of metres away from the mare. She was still trotting up and down the fence, looking for a way out. He started to talk to her, very quietly, in a soothing singsong voice. The watchers couldn't hear his words, but the mare seemed to. She stopped and turned to look at Seb, who continued talking. Ears twitching back and forth, she took a tentative step towards him. He held out his hand. She stretched her neck out and sniffed it, then took another step, and another. Only then did Seb rub her forehead and gently take hold of the rope. The watchers let out a collective sigh.

Sid, who'd managed to shepherd the other youngster into a stable, returned to the yard and wondered at the silence pervading it. Seb led the mare back to the trailer and handed her lead to Giles.

'All yours,' he said.

Giles gave the rope to Sid, looking angry, confused and embarrassed.

'Giles, darling, Charlie's going to show me where everything is in the house. You can manage without me, can't you?'

'Do as you like, Faye. I wouldn't want you to break old habits.'

Giles turned away to speak to the other groom.

As Seb led Faye through the house, she chattered away, though afterwards, he couldn't remember a thing she'd said. Eventually, Giles appeared. 'We can manage now, Proctor,' he said.

Seb gave a wry smile. 'Of course.'

This man has a huge problem, he thought. *Not only with his wife.*

Chapter 13

Seb settled into life at the local pub, while Sally settled into life at the Proctors'. Joan, who worked part-time, had to return to the Sunshine Coast, but Sally stayed with Alec and Connie. They had plenty of room, and Sally felt closer to Seb there, which made her more relaxed. She'd registered with the local medical centre and had driven her own car down, so she had freedom too. She often visited Caitlin, and they became close friends. Caitlin's two little ones were growing fast. Sally, who'd never had much to do with small children, was both fascinated and excited to think she'd soon have a baby of her own. She was still working part-time for the wine company via Zoom. Seb, however, found running his only real occupation. England's Covid numbers were soaring again, and there was talk of more lockdowns.

One evening, as he walked through the pub, he saw Sid sitting in the corner looking fed up. 'Hello, Sid. How's it going?'

Sid looked up with bloodshot eyes. It was plain he'd been there drinking for some time. 'Bloody hell,' he said. 'I thought you'd be gone by now.'

'I'm still waiting to get a repatriation flight. But what about you? You don't look very happy.'

'That bloody man! Heaven knows why he got the job. He has no idea how to handle the horses, so they all dislike him. Plus, his wife's a tart who cosies up to any man who shows his face – even me. How'd he get hired? Do you know?'

Seb sat down and chose his words carefully before he replied. It had been obvious to him that Giles had no real connection with horses, and Faye had made him uncomfortable.

'Well, the owner's in the Middle East, and I think he interviewed them by Zoom. It was probably quite difficult, doing it that way, and Giles would've been very convincing. I wonder what his CV is like. He could've faked it, I suppose.'

'Jesus, what a cock-up. The owner's going to end up with a stable full of nutty horses. I think I'll quit… I can't work there anymore. My wife loves the flat over the stables, so she'll be cheesed off. The other groom's in digs near here. She's a nice lass, but very green.'

'Sounds bad. I'm sorry.'

'Here, let me buy you a drink, mate. Us Aussie better stick together.'

Mentally, Seb squirmed. He didn't want to drink, and thought Sid had probably had enough, but in the end, he agreed to have a beer.

The two men sat and chatted for a time. Seb made his beer last, though Sid had a couple more. Apparently, Sid had started off as a jockey, with a promising career in front of him. However, he'd had a very bad fall when he was twenty. The horse in front of his fell, bringing his down too. His back had broken, as well as both legs. He'd been told he would never ride again. When he'd recovered enough, he became a travelling groom, flying with horses all over the world. Then he'd met his wife in England and settled down.

'I'd noticed you walked with a limp, and guessed it was horse-related,' Seb said. 'How old are you now?'

'Thirty-eight.'

'Oh.'

'I know. Everyone thinks I'm older. Look ancient, don't I?'

Seb was embarrassed. Sid did indeed look older.

'What's your story, then, mate?' Sid asked. Seb hated talking about himself, but Sid had been so open.

'Ten years ago, I was in a very bad place. Then I rescued an Arab mare, and we kind of healed each other. The rest is history, really.'

Sid looked at him curiously. 'Were horses a family business, then?'

Seb sat quietly for a minute, then said, 'My mother's father bred Arabs. Mum loved to ride but had given it all up when she met my father. Sorry, I can't tell you more – awful things have happened in my family, and now it's a closed book.'

'Shit happens in lots of families, Charlie, but if you don't want to talk about it, I understand. What I really want to know is how you got this extraordinary gift with horses.'

Seb grinned. 'To be perfectly honest, I'm not sure. They seem to understand that I love them and won't hurt them. It's about mutual trust, I think. Most horses I come across have been misused in some way, and it's really a case of letting them know I'll do them no harm.'

'Made that bastard look stupid the other day, didn't you?'

'It was never my intention to make anyone look stupid, Sid. I was concerned for the horse.'

'I reckon I'll give it a bit longer,' Sid said. 'Then, if another job turns up, I'm off. The missus will just have to put up with it. Trouble is, everything's pretty bad now, so God knows when that'll happen.'

Later, Seb sat in his room, mulling over what Sid had said. He just wished he'd left for Australia the moment he'd returned from France.

A few days later, more restrictions were imposed in the UK, as the virus once again took off. In Australia, Sally saw that the restrictions in England were tightening again, and it distressed her. Connie took her to see a doctor, who found her blood pressure was high. So now, a new worry reared its head. Sally was told to rest as much as possible; however, this only gave her more time to brood. It seemed a vicious cycle.

Alec, having repaired the ride-on lawnmower, waited for the man who'd brought it in to reappear, but no-one had seen hide nor hair of him. After making some enquiries, Alec found out that a tall, thin man had been to the dump and driven off with a broken mower. Of course, he couldn't be sure it'd been the same man, but he had a feeling it was. Why hadn't he returned, though? Who was he? Why had he come up with an elaborate plan to visit the workshop? Was he planning on stealing something? They had a lot of tools and machinery, but not much in the way of cash. Thinking back, Alec remembered how the man's gaze had continually strayed towards the house. What had that been about? One night, he lay awake, these thoughts going round and round in his head. He'd thought Connie was asleep, but turning his head, he saw her eyes glittering in the dark.

'What's up, love?' she said, quietly. 'Do you feel unwell?' Ever since Alec's brain tumour, she'd worried constantly about his health.

'I feel okay. Just mystified. You remember that odd bloke I told you about, who brought in a mower that wanted doing up and acted a little oddly? I think he may have got it from the dump.'

'Mm.' Connie was sleepy and only half-listening.

'He's never been back to collect it. I can't find out anything about him.'

'Maybe something's happened to him, and he hasn't been able to come back. I don't think it's worth lying awake over.'

'No, maybe not. Did I disturb you?'

Connie snuggled up to him. 'Only in a nice way. I think you need to put your mind to other things!'

Later, before he drifted off to sleep, Alec realised he hadn't told Connie what worried him most – that the man had seemed obsessed with looking at the house.

As the days passed, Sally was becoming more and more depressed. She was adamant that she wanted to stay with Connie and Alec, as she felt nearer to Seb there. Joan was happy; she didn't want anything untoward to happen. Sally was the last person in the world she would've thought would get so low, and they were all worried for her. Caitlin brought her little ones over when she could, and this always lifted Sally's spirits for a while, but she'd soon slump back into despair.

Then, on the first of October, they received good news: Seb had managed to get a flight home. He'd have to quarantine in a hotel for two weeks, so it'd still be over a month before he'd be with Sally and his family. The other issue was that his flight was into Sydney, not Brisbane, so if the border was shut, he'd still have to wait. It was frustrating, but at least he'd be on his way.

They all settled down to wait. Sally went up to spend time with her mother and brother, though she'd return to the Proctors' before Seb finally arrived. As she left their little road to join the bigger one, she caught a glimpse of a car parked in a driveway and had the strangest feeling she'd seen it before. She was also sure there was a man sitting in it. It gave her goosebumps, and she thought about ringing Connie to tell her. But by the time she'd driven a few kilometres down the road, she'd dismissed it as a figment of her oversensitive mind.

***

A few days later, Sid came looking for Seb at the pub. Seb had been out running all morning and was having lunch at the bar.

'Hey, mate, there you are,' Sid said. 'I just popped in to tell you I'm off – got a job in Wales. The missus isn't happy, but we're on the move, and it can't come soon enough for me.'

'That was quick. How'd you manage it?'

'A mate of mine put in a word for me. I'm sorry for the horses, but I reckon the family comes first.'

'Of course. Good luck – it was great to have met you.'

'You too. You're one extraordinary man. Wish I could've spent more time getting to know you.'

After Sid had gone, Seb sat contemplating what he'd said. He too felt sorry for the horses, who'd now just have Giles and an inexperienced groom to look after them.

Half an hour later, he was in his room when he heard a knock on the door. The landlord called out before Seb had a chance to answer it. 'Lady wants to see you downstairs.'

With that, Seb heard him walk away. He was a man of few words.

Seb's heart sank. He'd guessed who it was, and he was right; Faye Dean was waiting for him.

'Oh, Charlie! So good to see you.'

She made as if to kiss him, but Seb stepped back, with a muttered 'Social distancing.'

'Of course, I keep forgetting. Especially when I'm pleased to see someone.' He opened his mouth to speak, but she carried on talking. 'We wondered if you'd be so kind as to come and give us a hand. Those two young mares are quite difficult to handle!'

Seb was torn. He hated to think of any horse being upset, but he didn't want to be involved with the Deans. With the way Faye looked at him, he was sure she fancied her chances – and he was equally sure that Giles wouldn't be happy to see him.

'Giles wants me to come, does he?'

Faye hesitated. Seb watched emotions flit across her face. 'Well, no, he doesn't actually know I'm here. I... I thought to surprise him.'

'I'm sorry, but I'm leaving to return to Australia soon. Besides, I'm not sure your husband would want me to interfere.'

For a moment, Faye was silent. Seb could see her weighing up her words.

'My husband's actually frightened of horses,' she said, finally. 'He covers it up by being aggressive with them. His father's a trainer. Giles was expected to follow in his footsteps, but he had a horrible accident in his teens. It involved a horse, and now he can't get over his fear. This job's his last chance. If he fails, I don't know what we'll do. Please help – I'm sure you can.'

Now she'd been honest, Seb warmed towards her and even towards Giles. Seb had guessed fear was part of his trouble.

'I'm not sure I can help, but I'll come first thing tomorrow,' Seb heard himself say, even as part of his brain was saying *no, no, no!*

The next morning, Seb was as good as his word and ran out to the stables. Nothing looked very different from when he'd lived there, but then, it hadn't been long. Faye must've been watching for him, as the gate opened as he got there and closed behind him. She met him outside the stables.

'I didn't tell you yesterday that Sid had left, did I?' she asked.

'No, but I knew. He came and told me.'

'I rather thought he had. Giles and Wendy have just finished the morning feed, and they'll put the horses out soon. That always seems to cause trouble. We have some more mares arriving soon too.'

They started walking across the yard, just as Giles appeared, along with Wendy, the young groom. They were leading the two older mares, who seemed quite relaxed. Faye had warned Giles that Seb would be calling, so he just nodded as he walked past, but Seb could sense the currents of resentment and fear emanating from him. The mare he was guiding was up on her toes but not being silly.

It was a different matter when they led out the youngsters. Giles looked angry, his horse leaping about at the end of its lead rope. Wendy was having a real problem with her mare too. Seb stepped forward and spoke quietly to Wendy, who was obviously worried.

'Just relax and talk gently to her. She's young, like you, and excited to be going out in the paddock. Aren't you, girl?'

Wendy looked startled. The mare stopped pulling and looked at Seb with big, sorrowful brown eyes. Calming down, she let Wendy lead her out to the paddock without any more trouble, as Seb walked behind.

Once Wendy had let the horse go, she turned to Seb. 'How did you do that? She's always so difficult to let out and not much better when she comes in.'

'She's picking up on your nerves, which is making her nervous too. Just take deep breaths and keep calm. She'll get used to you being calm, then she will be too. Don't hang onto the lead rope, either; keep it long and loose. The tighter you hold it, the more she'll dance around. She thinks you expect her to play up, so she does.'

In the meantime, Giles had got his mare into the paddock and let her go. Now, he turned to Seb. 'Faye asked you to come, didn't she? Well, I don't want you here, so take yourself off and keep your nose out. Okay?'

Seb looked him in the eye for a moment, then turned away with a shrug. Faye, who'd been hovering nearby, stepped forward.

'Giles, let Charlie help you. if this job fails, we'll be in real trouble. I'm fed up with you having one job after another. Besides, you don't want to go back to your father cap in hand, do you?'

Giles's face crumbled, and he looked near tears. The three of them stood in awkward silence, until Seb spoke quietly.

'I know what fear is, Giles. I've been terrified many times in my life. Horses helped me overcome my unhappiness – I know they're the root of your trouble, but they can save you if you'll let them. Come on, let's have a look at that magnificent stallion you have, and see if we can make a start.'

With clear reluctance, Giles followed Seb back into the stables and up to the stallion's loose box. Seb entered the stall, talking quietly, then motioned for Giles to come in. The stallion laid his ears back, but with Seb whispering to him, he allowed Giles to halter him and lead him out. They spent some time in the yard, as Seb tried to show Giles how to gain the horse's trust. He soon realised it'd take all the time he had left in England to get Giles and the horses in a good place, but he was determined to help. It wasn't how he'd imagined spending his last couple of weeks in the country. In some ways, though, it made the waiting easier, and the black dog seemed to have left his shoulder for good. At least, he hoped it had.

In the end, Giles thanked Seb for his help. Faye did, too – though Seb kept as far away from her as he could.

Chapter 14

Eventually, Joe and Eve managed to get out of Victoria. They made it to Sydney, where they were again forced to stop, as it seemed unlikely the border with Queensland would open any time soon. Then, they heard Seb would be quarantining in Sydney, which consoled them in some ways.

Three weeks into October, Sally returned to the Proctors'. Since it was plain she'd be living there once the baby was born, she and Connie set about turning Sarah's old room into a nursery. Seb was on his way back, flying into Sydney, where he'd of course be going straight into hotel quarantine. They all hoped he'd be out by the time Sally gave birth.

Connie noticed Alec was very quiet. However, when she spoke to him about it, he brushed it off, saying he was just overwhelmed by excited women and baby talk. Connie wasn't convinced. She worried it was his tumour returning, although his demeanour was completely different to last time.

In reality, Alec was worried by the strange things that seemed to be happening around the place. He was sure someone had been in the yard at night, and once or twice, he'd thought he'd seen someone in the bushes by the property. He still had the old mower, and when he'd asked around, no-one had seemed to know anything about it, other than that it had been at the dump at some point. The more he thought about it, the more certain he became that the man had just been trying to have a nose around. As it happened, Alec had done a good job of restoring the mower. The engine was rather noisy, but it worked, and it certainly looked much better. However, he'd come to realise the bloke wasn't likely to return and claim it.

One afternoon, Alec decided to drive round the outlying properties and see if he could spot the ute the mower had arrived in. At first, it seemed he was out of luck, but finally, just off a little-used gravel road, he saw a rusty pickup by a dilapidated house. He parked in the driveway. As he walked closer, he became sure it was the same ute. He'd nearly reached it when the front door of the house opened, and an old man appeared.

'What d'you want? I ain't buying anything!'

'Sorry to intrude,' Alec said, 'but I was interested in the ute. It's yours, isn't it?'

'You a copper? If you are, you can get lost.'

Alec spread his hands wide. 'No, I'm nothing of the sort. I just thought I'd seen this ute before, but you weren't driving it.'

The man was bald and bent, with a long, scruffy beard. He looked very different to the person who'd come to the yard.

'I just want to speak to the man I saw driving it,' Alec said. 'There's nothing wrong – I have something that belongs to him, and I'd like to return it. Is he a friend of yours?'

'Friend?' The old man spat a glob of phlegm. 'The bugger owes me. He's no friend.'

'How come?'

Alec had walked closer, and wished he hadn't. The old man stank of sweat and stale tobacco, along with another fetid smell Alec didn't particularly want to identify.

'Turned up here a while back, in a fancy car like yours.'

Alec hid a smile. He had an old work car, which wasn't at all fancy.

'Asked if he could borrow the ute,' the old man continued. 'Said he'd pay some then, and a lot more when he brought it back. Had it a couple of days. Brought it back one night after dark, but by the time I got out here, he'd buggered off. Haven't seen him since. I'll kill the bastard if I do.' He spat again.

'Did he say what he wanted it for?'

'Nah, didn't say much worth remembering. You want to settle up for him?' The old man looked crafty all of a sudden.

Alec felt a wave of pity. This man lived in an isolated house that looked as if it would collapse in a puff of wind, seemingly on his own. Alec fished his wallet out and handed over a fifty dollar note. As he did so, he said, 'I just want to know what he's up to. I don't think it's anything good.'

The old man snatched the note from Alec, muttered something inaudible, then turned and went back into his house. Alec thought it might've been a thanks.

As he drove away, he reflected that he hadn't really learnt much, except that the stranger's ploy to get into the workshop had been very elaborate. He couldn't be too far away, but searching for him would be like looking for a needle in a haystack. Would it be worth approaching the police? But with what evidence? Alec doubted the old man would tell the police anything – he'd been hostile enough as it was. No, Alec would just have to keep his eyes open. He didn't trust the old man, but what he'd said made sense.

A few times, Connie also noticed a strange car in their little lane. She didn't think much of it, until a few days after Alec had found the ute. As she drove out onto the road, she saw a car parked up to her left, near the bushy area. She hesitated, wondering whether she should go and check it out.

Best not, she thought, glancing at her watch. *I'm late as it is.*

The man, who wasn't actually in his car, cursed himself again.

He was getting incredibly frustrated. He'd had no idea this was all going to be so strung out. He'd thought his plan would've been executed by now and it would've all been over, one way or another. He was tired of this game. It was beginning to feel fruitless, but surely he'd have resolution soon.

Just a little longer, he told himself.

***

The next day, the excitement in the Proctor household was palpable. Seb was back on home soil! Although he was in Sydney, on the other side of a closed border, he was at least in Australia – and he was in the same city as his grandparents, though it was unlikely they would get to see him.

Their first video call was very emotional. They all gathered round; Caitlin had come over without her children, as she'd thought they would be too distracting. Sally was the worst. She couldn't stop crying, partly from relief and partly from frustration. She was only a few weeks away from giving birth and wanted Seb to be there for it, but with the borders shut, it was looking less and less likely. Seb told her he'd apply for an exemption as soon as he was out of quarantine.

To his surprise, Seb was finding the situation very hard to cope with. He'd been sure that he'd be fine, once on home soil, even if he had to stay put for a couple of weeks. However, after only two days, the black dog had once more settled on his shoulder. He couldn't go out and run, and the food was unhealthy. Although he wasn't fussy, he'd been careful about what he ate for most of his life, because he'd wanted to keep fit for running. Many of the meals were things he'd normally avoid. He was like a caged beast and didn't know what to do with himself. At the same time, he didn't want to worry his family. Their regular calls were the only bright part of his day. Joe and Eve wanted to come to his hotel and stand outside to wave and shout hello, but Seb told them not to. He was afraid it would completely undo him.

Sally alternated between jubilation and despair. One minute, she was almost singing; the next, she was tearful and grumpy. She wasn't enjoying pregnancy and was worried that, in spite of his brave words, Seb would reject the child. Although she knew she was being unreasonable, she couldn't help herself. Her doctor had also warned her that her blood pressure was rising and advised her to take greater care and rest more, which she hadn't told anyone. Seb suggested she look for somewhere for them to live, with enough ground for a few horses, which took her mind off things for a short time. However, the lack of good options eventually only depressed her further. One thing they weren't worried about was money, as Seb had sold the place in England for a good price, and his business had been well in the black before the pandemic struck. So hotel quarantine, for example, wasn't a problem.

Time dragged. Connie was finding it hard to cope with Sally's mood swings, as the happy, sunny girl she'd met ten years before seemed to have completely disappeared over the last few weeks. Sally was over-the-top happy one minute and moody and grumpy the next. This was partially because she was desperate to see Seb.

Then, at last, the two weeks were up, and Seb met Joe and Eve. Their caravan was some distance outside Sydney, but they'd hired a unit in the city, which was where they reunited. Seb was shocked by how his grandmother had aged. She'd had cancer a couple of years ago, and though it was now in remission, it'd taken its toll. Joe, on the other hand, was hale and hearty. They were happy to see Seb. He looked as lean and fit as ever and happier than they'd seen him in ten years.

They held off hugging until they were inside Joe and Eve's hired unit. There, Eve took her grandson into her arms and cried a little. 'I was so afraid I'd never see you again, dear Seb. First I was ill, and you were in England. Then we were all stuck because of

Covid, then you were ill – then you couldn't get a flight back! It's a miracle you're here, it really is.'

Seb also had tears in his eyes. 'I know, Gran. I know. When Mum told me you had cancer, I nearly came home for a visit. I think I was afraid I wouldn't go back to England if I did. Funny thing is, I maybe wouldn't have met Sally again then.'

'Tell us how you met her again,' Joe said, 'and why you've changed your mind about... about everything.' He wasn't game to say having children, in case Seb had changed his mind. Before, he'd been so adamant that he hadn't wanted to be a father.

Seb related how he'd run into Sally. How he'd realised he never wanted to lose sight of her again, how they'd agreed to live together when he came home, how she'd phoned him and told him she was pregnant.

'I was so stunned. Sally was on the pill, after all. I just sat staring at the phone. I could hear that she was upset, but my heart started to race, and I suddenly realised it made perfect sense. It was my baby, my son or daughter. It was wonderful!'

Seb paused, embarrassed.

'Over the years, I've learnt something from horses,' he said, eventually. 'They're bad because of how they're treated, not how they're born. Even if they have a cranky parent, if they're treated right, they turn out well. I reckon our child will be the same.'

'Horses taught you that, Seb?' Eve asked.

'They've saved me in so many ways. I think I've saved a few of them too.'

Joe and Eve looked at each other.

'Great to have you home, son,' said Joe.

The next few weeks became a waiting game. Seb desperately tried to get an exemption to cross the border, but to no avail. Queensland Health didn't want to know about his circumstances.

It was very frustrating for everyone.

Towards the end of October, Sally and her mother arranged to meet for lunch in Brisbane. Joan had become very involved with charity work on the Sunshine Coast, so she was only planning to come down and stay with the Proctors for a few days after the baby was born. Connie would drive Sally to the station in Ipswich, then she'd take the train in. Connie would pick her up again later in the day. Joan and Sally were meeting at Roma Street and would have a general chat and get-together. Nothing major was planned.

As Sally sat on the train, her back began to ache, and she wriggled, trying to sit comfortably. When she got off at Roma Street, she could see her mother waiting for her. She put her hand up to wave.

Water poured down her legs. An enormous pain cramped her belly. She'd gone into premature labour.

Joan called 000, but the baby wouldn't wait, and lusty cries were coming from the back of the ambulance long before it reached the hospital. Although it'd arrived three weeks early, the baby was hale and hearty.

Sally had to stay in hospital for a while. When she rang Seb, he cried. For a moment, she was horror-struck, until he explained they were tears of joy. However, he was also frustrated, as he'd wanted to be there.

Three days later, Sally arrived back at the Proctors' with her new charge. The next morning, Alec took a mug of tea out to sit and enjoy the early sunshine, which had been part of his routine since his illness many years ago. He liked to sit there alone, in the peace and quiet. It put him in the right frame of mind to deal with the day. It was very early, just after five o'clock, and there, leaning against the veranda stairs, was a huge teddy bear. It was pale yellow and had a lovely benign expression. Alec searched around, but there was no note, nor any other indication of where the bear had come from. It was a complete mystery. No-one in the area owned up to buying it. The birth had been in the local paper, so Sally and the Proctors eventually assumed the gift was from a friend who didn't want to admit to it.

Over the next few weeks, Sally's frustrations grew and grew. Everyone worried about her. Her little son was very good, but she struggled to feel any great love for him, stifled by her postnatal depression. It wasn't something anyone had expected happy sunny Sally to suffer from, but really, it was all down to the frustration of not having Seb by her side.

'It's very well for them to say they're keeping us safe, but the mental health problem is going to be bigger than the Covid one, I think,' said Connie. All agreed with her, but the border also remained tightly shut, in spite of Seb's repeated attempts to get an exemption. He was continually on the phone with Sally. Soon, he realised he had to be careful to hide his own worries, as they'd only make her more distressed. On the upside, Sally was heartened by all the presents and good wishes that arrived for her and the baby, and very touched to get a call from Brianna.

'So, what's his name?' Brianna asked.

'Seb and I haven't really decided yet.'

'Is he a good baby?'

'Oh, Bri, he's gorgeous. He has a mop of blonde curls but big dark eyes like his dad. I didn't know babies could be born with so much hair!'

Brianna laughed. 'Nor did I, but Charlie is his father, so it doesn't surprise me.'

'I never really thanked you for looking after Seb when he was so ill. I—'

'No, stop, you don't need to thank me. I was glad to help. He's an extraordinary man... you're so lucky.'

Later, Sally sat looking down at her little son. Brianna was right. She was lucky in many ways. She'd found the love of her life and had a beautiful baby son, lovely parents-in-law, and no money troubles, at least for the moment. And yet, nothing had worked out as they'd planned. If only Seb were there to hold his little son! Then, everything would be alright. Sally was overcome by a wave of frustration.

In Sydney, Seb was feeling much the same. It didn't matter whom he spoke to; they just told him he wasn't eligible for an exemption and would have to wait until the border reopened. His mental health mattered not one jot to them, although they kept talking about it and saying they were keeping Queenslanders safe. But were they? Safe from the virus, maybe, but not from mental illness. No-one seemed to care about Seb's mental health.

Sally decided she needed air, having made herself miserable. She put the baby Proctor in his stroller, called out to Connie that she was going for a walk, and set off. She turned right out of their driveway. Ever since her fright on her walk with Pip, she'd avoided going left, even in the car. When she got to the end of the lane, she turned left, not wanting to walk into town. It was a prettier route, and it was getting hot, though it was still early. She wouldn't go too far. As she walked, she was aware of a car pulling up behind her, but thought nothing of it until she heard footsteps approaching. She turned to see a tall, bearded man with a large Akubra shadowing much of his face.

'Sorry to bother you. I just wanted to know if this is the road up to Mount French,' he said rapidly, staring into the stroller. 'What a lovely baby. What's its name?'

Sally felt slightly uncomfortable. 'You're on the wrong side of town for Mount French. And he doesn't have a name yet.'

'That's sad. Why not?'

'His dad's stuck over the border, so when he gets here, we'll decide on one.'

The stranger bent down closer to the stroller, then straightened.

'Gorgeous little chap. Thank you,' he said, before turning and almost running back to his car.

He was feeling just as frustrated as everyone else. It was too soon to show himself, but all this had taken forever, and he didn't have long to finish what he'd started. That little boy, though... he was gorgeous. He wondered what Connie thought of her grandson and, even more importantly, what Seb would think when he saw his child. What would he be called? The thoughts swirled round and round in his head.

Sally frowned. He seemed familiar, somehow, but his behaviour had certainly been strange. She also felt that she'd seen his car somewhere before. Still, she decided not to mention it to Connie or Alec. They might think she had an overactive imagination, especially as they were all struggling with the family's separation. However, when her son woke for a feed in the middle of the night, she realised where she'd seen the man before.

'Well, little one,' she whispered, as he guzzled away at her breast, 'I think he stopped to help when my car was playing up all those weeks ago. He must be a local. But then again, he can't be, or he'd know where Mount French is. I'm sure they had the same voice, and they were both tall, although the one before didn't have a beard. Maybe they're related!'

Sally sat musing, until she remembered – *the car!* It'd had a New South Wales numberplate, she was sure of it. Then another thought occurred to her. Was he stalking her? Had it been him hiding in the bushes when she'd gone for a walk? She shivered at the thought. Yet, in some ways, he hadn't felt threatening. She didn't know why, but in her bones, she didn't think he meant her any harm. Then again, people got murdered by people they trusted, so maybe she should worry. But why? Surely he wasn't interested in her. Why would he be, when the only time he'd spoken to her was when her car had had a problem? As her thoughts cartwheeled round and round, she realised the baby had dozed off. She roused him and put him to her other breast, but he only suckled for a short time, and it wasn't long before they were both asleep.

The next morning, when she walked into the kitchen, Alec stopped talking so abruptly she knew she'd interrupted something private.

'Sorry, I—'

'Come and sit down, Sal,' Connie said. 'I think you need to hear this. Doesn't she, Alec?'

'Yes, I suppose. I just didn't want to worry the two of you.'

Alec told them about the odd behaviour of the man who'd brought in the mower, and how it'd plainly been a ruse to come into the workshop and he seemed hard to trace. As Sally sat listening, her heart began to race. 'Was he tall and lean?'

'Yes. He had a beard, but his hat was pulled down, so I couldn't see much of his face.'

'I think I've met him twice!'

'What? How?' Connie sounded scared. Alec also looked very worried. Sally told them about the time he'd offered to help with her car and about their encounter the day before, when she'd decided it was the same person.

'He didn't threaten you in any way?' Alec asked.

'No. He just admired the baby, asked his name, then took off.'

'And you're sure it was the same man?'

'The more I think about it, the more certain I am. His car was the same, too, and had a New South Wales numberplate. I didn't notice what make it was, or its actual number, but it was dark blue and fairly new.'

Connie and Alec exchanged a glance.

'I don't like the sound of this at all, Con.'

'But it's been months since Sally's car broke down and months since he brought that old mower. Surely, if he was a threat to us, he would've done something by now.'

'Mysterious all round,' Sally said. 'What about the teddy bear? You haven't found out who left it?'

Alec and Connie both shook their heads.

'You don't think it was our mystery man, do you?' Sally asked.

'Why on Earth would he?' Connie asked. 'And anyway, how would he know who you were and that you'd had the baby?'

'Well, Con, you did put the birth in the local paper,' Alec said.

'Yes, but that aside, why would he? None of us know him. It doesn't make any sense.'

They talked round and round in circles, but eventually agreed it was no good going to the police. They would wait and see what happened next.

Chapter 15

The month passed slowly. Seb was aware he'd been very lucky, as there were still thousands of Australians stuck overseas. As far as he could see, no government had any real plan in place, and if they did, it seemed unrealistic. Still, to be so near and yet so far was incredibly hard, and nobody seemed to understand him. Joe and Eve said they did, but Seb didn't believe them. The time he'd spent with Sally had been so brief it sometimes seemed like a dream. Getting back to her and holding his baby felt more important by the day. He hadn't expected that even after his quarantine was over, he'd still be unable to be with them. It seemed incredibly cruel. Running was the only thing that kept him sane.

Alec and Connie were worried about Sally, as she seemed preoccupied. In fact, she was worrying about the stranger.

'Not long until Christmas,' Caitlin announced, as she arrived one day with her children in tow. Alec and Connie were relieved that she and Sally had become such good friends, as they felt it was the one thing preventing Sally from collapsing in a heap.

'God, I can't think about that,' Sally said. 'What will I do if the borders aren't open by then? I can't bear to think of it.'

Caitlin put her arms around Sally. Caitlin too was worried about her; she almost seemed a stranger sometimes and was very moody.

'Sal, why don't you let me look after the baby tomorrow? You can express milk, then go Christmas shopping in Brisbane with Mum. What do you say?'

Sally smiled for the first time that day. 'Would you? We could leave it until next week and go the day before the border opens – if they keep their promise and open it. I could get Seb a really nice present. Once he's home, I don't want to leave his sight!'

So it was arranged. Sally suddenly felt happier, though she was terrified that the border wouldn't open, that the powers who decided these things would play a trick, and she and Seb wouldn't get together. That evening, during their usual call, he pointed out that they really needed to name the baby and suggested the name Martin.

Sally rolled it around her tongue a few times. 'Why?'

'I dunno, really. It just popped into my head. And we could give him the middle name Joe, after my grandfather – Martin Joe Proctor.'

'Okay, but why not Joe Martin Proctor?'

'Maybe... oh, then we could call him JP!'

Sally laughed. 'I like it, I really do.'

So they agreed he was to be called Joe or JP for short. 'It can be the first thing we do when I get there,' said Seb. 'Register his birth.'

'The *first* thing? I had a better idea.'

'You have a point. It'll be the second thing, then. I can't wait, darling. One part of me badly needs attention. I can't say more, or I think Granny Eve will hear!'

Sally giggled. It felt good; she hadn't laughed much lately. 'Only a few more days, Seb.'

Seb and his grandparents were busy getting themselves organised for the drive north. They soon heard there would be long queues at the border. Seb didn't care – he just wanted to get there.

The next day, Connie and Sally dropped baby Joe off at Caitlin's. It was still early, but the mercury was climbing. Shortly after they left, Caitlin put JP out on the back veranda, where there was a good breeze blowing. He'd had a good feed and she knew he would sleep for a while. With a net over the stroller and her just inside, she was confident all would be well. She busied herself in the kitchen, making chocolate chip cookies, with her children helping or hindering – she wasn't sure which. Then Emma fell off her stool and hurt her arm. Between cuddling her and sorting out the general mess, Caitlin didn't check on JP for about twenty minutes.

Looking out, she gasped. The net was off the stroller. She rushed outside, her heart racing. There was no sign of the baby. Just a note lying where JP had been.

He is safe with me. DO NOT CALL THE POLICE. This is a family matter. I just need to see his grandmother and father. M. W.

'Oh my god!' Caitlin heard herself scream, which set her two children off. With shaking hands, she managed to ring her mother after several attempts.

For several moments, Caitlin couldn't form her words properly, and Connie couldn't understand what she was saying. Then, finally, she got it. Sally was in a changing room, and Connie had come out to put back a dress, which gave her a chance to think calmly.

'Take the children and go to your dad. He'll look after you until we get back. For now, we'll do as the note says and not call the police.'

'But – but Mum!'

Connie took a deep breath. From the contents of the note,

she'd guessed the Windemere family was involved. How, though, she wasn't sure.

'Caitlin, please do as I say. I have Sally to deal with. Don't make it harder.'

When Sally emerged, she didn't need to be told there was trouble. One look at Connie's face was enough.

'What is it? Is it JP? Seb? What?'

Connie took the clothes draped over Sally's arm and hung them on a rack nearby. 'We have to go. Now. Just give me a minute, and I'll tell you.'

Sally, though white as a sheet, had the sense to wait while Connie steered her towards the lift to the car park. Once in the lift, she opened her mouth to speak, but Connie beat her to it.

'Look, JP has been abducted, possibly by a relative of mine.'

Sally trembled, tears streaming down her face. 'Oh, God. God! What will we do?'

Gently, Connie took her by her shoulders. 'Sal, you've got to be brave. Going to pieces won't help. We have to keep calm. The man left a note, saying JP is safe. It's Seb and me he wants to speak to. Hopefully, we can resolve this soon.'

Shortly afterwards, they were on their way home. The journey had never seemed so long, and apart from Sally crying, it was spent in complete silence.

Chapter 16

When Caitlin arrived at the Proctors' house, she rushed down to the workshop and burst in, crying, 'Dad, Dad!'

'Cat, darling, whatever is the matter?'

In between sobs, Caitlin managed to tell Alec what had happened. Alec immediately knew it had something to do with the mysterious man he'd seen.

Caitlin showed him the note. A little calmer now, she said, 'We must call the police. They'll know what to do.'

'No, Connie won't want the police involved if it's to do with her family, and somehow, I rather think it is,' he said. 'She's had enough of the police before – she hates the media stuff that goes with it. The *W* in the signature makes me think it's a Windemere, but we'll see when she gets back. We have to keep calm. Where are your two?'

'Still in the car. God, they'll be roasting.'

After retrieving the children, they all went into the house. It was a hot day and a relief to put the aircon on. Caitlin had parked the car in the shade and had only been a few minutes, but she felt bad that she'd left the children, as they were both distressed. Emma especially was very red-faced. Both children had picked up on their mother's emotions, and once inside, they were both a little cranky. Alec made Caitlin sit down and brought her a glass of whisky.

'You need brandy, really, but we don't have any. Get this down, and you'll feel better. You've had a shock.'

'Dad, I feel so guilty. Sally left Joe with me. How could I have let this happen? I was cooking with Emma here, and Alec was sitting on the floor playing. Joe was just outside the door in the stroller, and I didn't hear a thing.'

'This man must be very stealthy. I think he might've left that teddy bear – I was surprised Pip didn't bark, because he must've come very close to put it on the steps.'

'But what does he want with Mum, even if he is a relative? Why not just approach her normally? Why all this, and why does he want to see Seb? That must be who he means.'

Alec shook his head. He thought he might know the answer, but he couldn't be sure.

'When will he get in touch?' Caitlin asked. 'If he does, that is. Oh, this is a nightmare.'

Although Alec was struggling with his own inner turmoil, his priority was to keep Caitlin and his grandchildren calm. He had his work cut out for him, with Caitlin quiet one minute and crying the next, so he was very relieved when Connie and Sally finally pulled up outside. However, Sally immediately rushed in and shouted at Caitlin for letting JP be taken. It took Alec and Connie a while to soothe both young women, and of course, the shouting had upset the children again.

Sally and Caitlin were both a mess. After disappearing for a few minutes into another room, Alec returned and took Caitlin's hand. 'I've rung Bob. He'll get the next flight home; you need him right now.' Turning to Sally, he said, 'Seb and my parents are on their way to the border. Hopefully, they'll cross tomorrow, and he'll be here soon after. Right now, we need to—'

A phone rang, making them all jump. It was Alec's work mobile.

'What?' he asked, as he answered the call, thinking it was one of his workers. 'I'm busy.'

He stopped speaking. The others watched emotions flit across his face, then he handed the phone to Connie without a word.

'Hello?' she asked.

For a few seconds, there was silence. Then a male voice spoke.

'Connie, I'm sorry I took the baby, but I was afraid you wouldn't see me otherwise. I need to see you and your son, just the two of you. I won't let any harm come to the baby. I'll take great care of him, but it is imperative that I meet you both. Don't call the police. It won't help and might be dangerous. Meet me at the top of Mount French, in the car park, at 10.30 tomorrow morning.'

'Wait, Seb isn't here – he's stuck over the border. Is this Maurice?'

The phone went dead.

Connie was shaking and white as a sheet. She sank into a nearby chair, putting her head into her hands. Alec sat on the arm and rubbed her back.

For a while, no-one said anything. Alec got up and started to make drinks, and eventually, they were all sitting around the table drinking tea. Emma and young Alec were both fractious. Still, no-one spoke; they didn't know what to say. Alec got to his feet and left the room again. They could all hear him talking on the phone. Apart from the two children, it was as if they were all struck dumb. Even Sally was quiet.

Eventually, Alec came back. 'Both Sarah and Joan are on their way,' he said. 'I think you need your mum, Sally, and Sarah should be here too. They'll both arrive this evening. Cat, you can stay with us until then. Or do you want to go home and wait there?'

Just then, Caitlin's phone rang. It was Bob, who said he'd managed to get a flight home and would be back in a few hours.

Sally felt a fleeting burst of jealousy. Everyone seemed focused on Caitlin when it was her baby who'd been abducted. She opened her mouth to speak, but a large sob escaped instead.

Caitlin turned and gathered Sally in her arms. 'Oh, I'm so very sorry. If only—'

'Come now, you two,' Connie said. 'This isn't the time for recriminations. We have to focus on how we're going to play this.'

Connie had got her strength of character back. For a time, all the old nightmares of her desperately unhappy childhood had invaded her mind. Now, however, she was fighting them back, determined not to let them overwhelm her or her family.

Her words had the desired effect. Caitlin said she'd take her exhausted children home, and Sally also calmed down, though she was still very tearful.

'Should we let the police know, Con?' asked Alec, once Caitlin had gathered herself and departed with the children.

'I don't want them involved – sorry, Sally.' Sally had made a noise of disbelief. 'If we call them, it'll open a whole new can of worms. He said not to contact the police, and for now, I think we should comply. It's not in his interest to harm the baby, and I don't think he's a violent person.' As she said this, Connie mentally crossed her fingers. 'Hopefully, by this time tomorrow it'll be over, and Baby Joe will be back in your arms. So too will Seb.'

'But what about JP's food and nappies and everything? And look at me, I'm leaking milk all over the place.'

'We'll get the breast pump working, for a start. Let's hope Maurice, if it is him, had the forethought to prepare everything JP needs. Maybe he has had his own children and knows what he's doing. I really don't think he'll harm JP. If I did, I'd be dialling 000 right now.'

'But why has he done this?' Sally asked. 'How's he related to you? How did this happen?' All these questions flooded out of her mouth, while she did as Connie suggested and pulled out the breast pump.

'Maurice – at least, I assume it's Maurice – was adopted by my grandparents when he was about nine or ten, after his parents were killed in a car crash. I think they were members of my family's church. My father, who was quite a lot older than Maurice, didn't like him, so we only saw him rarely. When I was in my teens, he'd turn up and watch us with the horses. He and I only ever spoke in passing. I knew he liked me, but it wasn't something I really thought about. Then he and Dad had a row, and we never saw him again. Quite frankly, the memories are very vague. I've never delved too deeply into that part of my life. I had to, when… well, you know when, but I try not to dwell on it, and I reckon I'm on top of all the bad memories now. Or at least I was. Why has the bastard turned up now, just as Seb was feeling better? Why has he done this? It beggars belief.' Tears streamed down Connie's cheeks, as her bad memories resurfaced once again. She and Sally clung to each other. It was going to be a long night.

Shortly afterwards, the landline went. It was Seb. He was very distressed, and although he'd phoned ahead to try to jump the queue, he'd got nowhere. Sally was a mess speaking to him. All she could do was cry, so Connie took over to explain the situation.

'Look, sweetheart, we're quite certain Maurice Windemere has taken JP. He says he means baby Joe no harm, and somehow, I believe him. I think it's just a means of meeting with you and me. Why is anyone's guess, but it must be to do with the past. You were strong and brave before, in Victoria, and you must be again. Sally isn't coping, so it's you and me, okay? I don't want the police involved. Last time, it just added to all the drama, especially when the press got hold of it.'

Seb took a big breath. 'I understand, Mum, but what if it all goes wrong?'

'I'll take the blame, so it had better not. If it does, though, we'll get the police involved. I just hope Maurice is as good as his word.'

'Can you be sure it's him? After all, you haven't seen him in over thirty years.'

'Something about his voice... yes, I'm sure.'

'Well, we're getting nearer to the front of the line, so hopefully we'll be with you in the morning. We'll drive through the night if necessary. Love you, Mum. I'll speak to Sal again now.'

Sally made a big effort, and this time was calmer. She was pleased to think Seb would be there soon. That thought was helping her through the nightmare; she also trusted Alec and Connie and hoped their judgement was correct. Later, when she was lying down, resting, the fog of panic cleared from her brain a little, and she remembered the tall man she'd seen before. Immediately, she went in search of Connie.

'Connie, Connie – it's the same man, isn't it? The one we talked about before. The strange man who brought the mower to Alec and spoke to me about Mount French.'

'What did he say? I can't remember what you told us.'

'That first time, he just asked whether I needed help. The second time, just recently, he said JP was a lovely baby, or something like that. I didn't feel threatened, but it was bizarre. He had a full beard and an Akubra pulled down low, so I couldn't really see his face.'

'You said he looked familiar, didn't you?' Connie asked. 'In what way?'

Sally put her head on one side. 'I'm not really sure, but he just seemed like someone I'd met before. That isn't possible, though, is it?'

Connie, who had a feeling she knew what it was all about, just shook her head. She didn't feel at all well, but she wasn't going to let anyone see that, least of all Sally.

That evening, Joan arrived. There were more tears. She was angry with Caitlin for letting JP be taken, and even with Sally and Connie for leaving him in the first place. She knew she was being unreasonable but couldn't control it. It had a positive result, however, as Sally grew defensive of Caitlin and Connie.

'None of us could've foreseen this, Mum,' she said, when they were alone on the veranda. 'Caitlin blames herself enough without you having a go at her. Don't be like this. It's making everything harder.'

Joan sank down onto a nearby chair. 'Why haven't you called the police?' She fumbled with her bag, searching for her phone.

'Connie said not to. She's had a hard time with the police before. Besides, she thinks she can deal with this.'

'Tosh. I'm calling them now.'

Connie came out onto the veranda. 'Don't, Joan. It'll make things worse. I know what I'm dealing with, and the note the kidnapper left said not to contact the police. Here, read it.' She held the note out.

Joan hardly glanced at it and drew out her phone. Sally glanced from her to Connie. Then, before either could react, she snatched the phone from her mother's hand.

'Are you mad, Mum? The note says no police. Until we know what we're dealing with, I, for one, will go along with that. Connie says she can sort it, and I don't want to jeopardise JP's life. For God's sake, he is *my* baby, mine and Seb's. I'll do anything to get him back.'

Joan was shocked. She and Sally had always been so close, but the last months had changed something within them both. Another symptom of the awful Covid pandemic.

'Sally, darling, I'm only trying to help. Don't forget that he's my grandson too.'

'I know, but please do this the way Connie wants. I trust her, and so does Seb.'

Joan shrugged. She wasn't happy, but she would go along with it, if that was what Sally wanted. 'Well, let's hope this man knows how to look after a baby.'

'I hope so too.'

They ate a scratch supper, or rather pretended to, as no-one felt like eating. Joan and Sally both went to bed early, though neither of them would sleep.

Alec and Connie sat at the table. 'Alec, I'm sorry my relatives have caused you so much trouble. I really thought we'd got through it all. Who would've thought of Maurice Windemere turning up after all these years?'

'Why do you think he's turned up, Con?'

'Why do you?'

'Well, let's wait and see.'

Connie nodded. She didn't want to open Pandora's box until she had to. She'd believed it was firmly shut, but now it seemed otherwise. She was dreading the confrontation she knew was happening tomorrow and hoped against hope that baby Joe would be looked after.

Seb was a mess, sitting in a long line of cars and caravans, waiting to cross the border. Would he ever get to hold his son, or would this monster make it impossible? Memories of his grandfather Saul surfaced, and his blood ran cold. Why had this man come back to haunt them? What possible motive could he have?

Chapter 17

The next morning, Connie was first in the kitchen, making both tea and coffee for anyone who wanted a drink. Shortly after, Sally appeared. It was plain she hadn't slept. Her eyes were swollen, and she was so pale that her skin seemed almost translucent.

'Sally, sweetheart, come and sit down.'

Sally slumped at the table. 'I wanted to look special for Seb, and I couldn't look much worse,' she said, tears welling in her eyes.

'Sweetheart, Seb won't notice. All he'll want is you and baby Joe to be safe and sound. He won't care about anything else.'

Joan stepped into the kitchen. She didn't look much better than Sally.

'Tea or coffee?' Connie asked her. 'I was going to make toast too. I don't think any of us feel like eating much.'

Joan sat next to Sally. 'Tea, thanks. What time are we meeting this man?'

'Sorry, it'll be just Seb and me,' Connie said.

'But surely I can—'

'Mum! Please don't do this, it's all bad enough as it is. Let Connie do what she thinks is best. I'll be going, but I'll wait in the car. I want you to stay here. I'm so glad you came, but please don't rock the boat and make things worse.'

Joan stared at her daughter, conflicting emotions flitting across her face. Connie felt sorry for her. It had nothing to do with her, but she'd been dragged into the legacy of Connie's dysfunctional family. Sitting down on her other side, Connie put an arm around her shoulders.

'Look, Joan, this is all my fault in a way. I'm fairly sure I know who's taken JP, and I might even know why. I don't want to tell you yet, but it's me he wants – me and Seb. He won't harm the baby.'

Please let that be true, Connie thought. Even if she was right about Maurice, why would he go to such lengths to speak to her and Seb?

Seb! Hopefully he'd soon be with them.

***

Seb, Joe, and Eve were having problems of their own. They'd got across the border and had taken the inland route to get to Boonah, rather than the longer but easier Logan Motorway. Just after Canungra, their Landcruiser had had a massive blowout. Joe wrestled with the car as the steering went, and the caravan started to snake from side to side. Finally, he managed to pull up on the side of the road. But it was a very hazardous place – narrow, and just past a blind corner.

Seb jumped out and put their little warning signs up. As he walked back to the car, he saw the caravan also had a flat tyre. It wouldn't be easy to fix everything. Their luck was good in another way, though, as just at that moment, a police car came round the corner and stopped, seeing their predicament. The three of them were very relieved, as from then on, they didn't have to worry that they'd cause an accident.

Looking at his watch, Seb knew he was going to be late. He

said nothing to Joe and Eve, as they were stressed enough, but walked away and rang Sally.

'Sal, are you okay? Look, we've had a blowout. We're alright, but... darling, don't cry. I'm not far away now.'

Sally, gulping back tears, said she'd hand the phone to Connie. Seb quickly told his mother what'd happened.

'I'll get your dad to come and get you,' Connie said. 'He can bring you straight to the meeting place. Now, where exactly are you?'

Seb told her, and she organised for Alec to pick him up. Immediately, Sally wanted to go along.

'Don't see why not,' Alec said. 'They can have a reunion before we meet this man.'

Connie nodded slowly. 'I suppose that'll work. Sally, get ready to go.'

For the first time in twenty-four hours, Sally smiled fleetingly, then rushed away to get ready.

'Something else is troubling you, Con. I can see it in your face.'

'It's just that Joan's going to be stuck here alone now, and I'm not sure that's a good thing.'

'Why don't you drop her at Caitlin's as you go? She won't be on her own then.'

'I don't know... she was so angry with Caitlin. I don't want there to be any more trouble.'

'Ring Cat and see what she says. After all, Sarah is there, and so is Bob, so it should be fine.'

Sally appeared, looking better than earlier, though she was still emanating waves of stress and fear. She called out to her mother as she left the house. Joan didn't answer.

When Sally and Alec had left, Connie went to find Joan. She

was sitting on a bench under the old jacaranda tree. Like Sally, she looked pale and worn-out. As Connie approached, she glanced up, and Connie saw that she'd been crying.

'Oh, Connie, what's going to happen? Do you think JP is alright? Will this man hand him back without trouble?'

Connie sat down beside her and took her hand. 'Look, if I thought for one second that little Joe was in danger, I'd be the first one to call the police. I certainly wouldn't react the way I have. I'm sure my father's adopted brother has the baby, and I remember him as a gentle soul, though it's been over thirty years since I last saw him. I think he just wants to meet and talk, though I have to admit it's a strange way of going about it. But then, my family always has been strange.'

'He wasn't involved with you much, was he? I don't remember his name being mentioned before. What does he want from you and Seb?'

Connie shifted on the seat, uncomfortable. She wasn't sure what Maurice wanted, though she had a good idea, and it wasn't something she wanted to relive.

She squared her shoulders. She just had to get through this, for everyone's sake.

'I really don't know for sure, Joan. Let's wait and see. But more to the point, are you okay?'

'Not really. I still miss Ben, my husband, like mad. He was too young to die. Then, just before Alec rang to tell me about JP, I heard my brother-in-law is in hospital with Covid down in Victoria. It's not looking good. It just goes on and on, this Covid thing, and no-one seems to have a clear idea of how it'll all pan out. There are thousands of Aussies stuck abroad. How did Seb manage it?'

'He flew with some horses to Singapore as a groom, then managed to get a flight home from there. It took some organising, and wasn't quite within the rules, strictly speaking, but the important thing is that he made it. Now, what do you want to do, Joan? I'm not happy leaving you here alone when you're feeling upset. I suggest you go to Caitlin's – she and Sarah will look after you.'

Joan's eyes flooded with fresh tears. 'I was so horrible to her yesterday. I know she didn't do anything wrong.'

Connie patted her shoulder. 'She'll understand, and I rather think she's beating herself up more than any of us. Come on, time to get organised.'

Both women stood.

'We just have to cope with the here and now,' Connie said. 'Once we've got this all sorted, then we'll look to the future. They're saying we'll have a vaccine rollout soon, so fingers crossed.'

Connie didn't ring Caitlin. She just drove Joan to the house and, leaving Joan in the car, went in to see her daughters. The house was bustling with Caitlin's two, Sarah, and Bob, who'd just arrived.

'Of course we'll look after her,' Caitlin said, after Connie had told them how upset Joan was. She went straight out to the car. 'Come on in, Joan, and meet my husband and my sister. She's the clever one – and the kids aren't cranky today, they're just being spoilt.'

After leaving Joan with Caitlin and her family, Connie set off to meet Alec and Seb with her heart in her mouth.

Chapter 17

Sally, sitting beside Alec on the way to pick Seb up, found she was a bundle of nerves. *Why?* she asked herself, silently. *He loves me. Why am I nervous?*

Alec glanced across at her.

'Got butterflies?'

'Yes. How did you know?'

'Well, you'd have to be made of stone to not be worried, excited, scared... I feel the same with all this going on, and I'm just a man!'

Sally smiled. 'You may not be Seb's biological father, Alec, but he's a lot like you.'

Taking his hand off the steering wheel, Alec patted her knee, and she knew he'd been moved by her words. The bond between him and Seb was very strong – stronger than many father-son relationships.

At last, they reached a queue of traffic, and Alec rightly guessed it was caused by Joe and Eve's stranded car. He stopped on the side of the road. 'Wait here, love. I'll go and get Seb.'

As soon as he left the car, he was enveloped in a bear hug. Seb had been watching for them. Then Sally leapt out, and the three of them stood there, arms around each other, crying and laughing at the same time. Several cars honked their horns as they drove slowly past. None of the three were sure whether it was to tell them off or to applaud them.

Finally, they broke apart.

'Come on, then,' Alec said. 'We have to go meet your mum and little son.'

'Yes, let's go. Granny and Grandad said they'd catch up later.'

Alec felt guilty about not waiting to speak to his parents, but they all knew it was most important to deal with the problem at hand. 'I'll see them soon,' Alec said to Sally, as he looped a nifty U-turn through a space in the traffic.

Alec kept looking at Seb in the rear-view mirror. He seemed taller and leaner than he had almost six years ago. His hair, which he'd always worn longer than most, was streaked with grey, though it only added to his good looks. His eyes were sparkling with the joy of being with Sally again; however, as they got closer to Mount French, Alec could feel the tension building. Seb and Sally were holding hands tightly, but they weren't speaking, the atmosphere taut enough to cut with a knife.

They started on the road up to Mount French. It seemed to Sally to go on and on forever, uphill and down, with fewer and fewer houses as they neared the summit. When they reached the national park sign, they saw Connie's car pulled over to one side. After they all got out, Seb and Connie hugged long and hard.

'Good to see you, Mum.'

Connie blinked tears from her eyes. It wasn't the time for crying. 'You'd better come with me now. Alec, park nearby, but try not to spook Maurice.'

'You're sure it's Maurice?' Seb asked.

'I can't think who else it would be, and I worry why he's done this – but come on, we'll know soon.'

As she and Seb drove further up the road, they saw an increase in cars and people.

'Since school's finished for summer, I can't think why he chose here,' Connie said. 'It'll be busy.'

'Maybe that's the idea. He could feel safer when there are others about.'

'I hardly think you and I are a threat to anyone, do you?'

Seb shook his head. Growing up, he'd always felt closer to Alec, but his encounter with Connie's parents had made him reassess that. He was close to his mother too. However, he refused to think of Connie's parents as his grandparents; that thought was too awful to contemplate.

Noticing a parking spot, Connie pulled over, while Alec drove on a little further. She couldn't see anyone waiting for them, but the trees and crowds of people provided plenty of hiding spots. She got out of the car, followed by Seb.

'Connie,' said a voice behind them.

They both spun round. Connie's hand flew to her mouth, and she gasped, 'Oh my God.'

Seb, too, was frozen to the spot. It was like looking at a much older image of himself. They were the same height and had the same hair, and even the same way of moving.

Seb recovered first. 'Where is my son?'

Maurice indicated a car not far away. 'He's asleep. Don't worry, he's fine.'

Ignoring him, Seb strode across to it. Baby Joe was sound asleep in a car seat in the back. Seb's heart contracted as he took in the chubby face and smattering of blonde hair, like Sally's, or his mother's. He opened the unlocked door and gently undid the harness. JP made a face in his sleep, then opened his eyes, looking at his father for the first time.

'Hello, mate. You okay? Come on, let's find your mummy.'

'She's here.'

Sally was behind Seb. She'd been looking on from a distance and had run across as soon as she'd seen him go to the car. He turned and placed JP in Sally's arms, then kissed the baby's head.

'Take him home, Sal, while I deal with that bastard.'

He kissed Sally briefly then walked back to where Connie and Maurice were standing watching him. A few times, Maurice had started to speak, but Connie had put her hand up, signalling that he wait.

As Seb approached, she said, 'Maurice, you got us here in a very cruel and unnecessary way. What do you want?' She was shaking but trying to keep her cool.

'I want to explain – to put things right before it's too late.'

'It's already too late. Far too late. You must realise that. I know now it was you, you who—'

Connie couldn't finish. Again, she saw her horse's ears silhouetted in gold against the lake, as she rode in the early morning. She remembered the runner who'd been crouching by the track. Remembered dismounting to help, then waking up in hospital with a massive headache, sore between her legs. Remembered her father saying it was all her fault and shooting her beautiful horse in front of her.

Connie jolted back to the present. Tears were streaming down her face, and Seb was speaking.

'So, you're the bastard who raped my mother. I may look like you, but I sure as hell hope I'm nothing like you. What do you want, after thirty odd years? What do you think to gain from all this?'

Connie was shivering uncontrollably. Through chattering teeth, she said, 'Say what you want to say, then leave us alone.'

Seb put his arm around her shoulders. 'Mum, it's okay.' He glared at Maurice, jaw tense. 'Look what you've done.'

'I'm truly sorry. If only I could explain... maybe you'd feel better, Connie. Please, let me explain. I can't go away until I have.'

Connie looked at him directly for the first time. He was so like Seb, in some respects, though very different in others. If she listened now, maybe he'd leave them alone.

'You'd better come to my car. I need to sit down.'

They made their way to Connie's car, Seb supporting his mother, who was trembling and walking like an old woman. When they reached it, Seb took the keys from his mother, who was still shivering uncontrollably. Alec, who'd been waiting nearby, jumped out of his car.

'Con!' he called.

'It's okay,' Seb said. 'Take Sal and JP home. We'll be there soon.'

Alec hesitated. Even from a distance, he could see that Connie was very upset. 'But...'

'Please, Dad. I'll look after her.'

Quite a few people in the car park were intrigued by the scene playing out. A crowd was gathering. Seeing this, and knowing Seb would take care of his mother, Alec went back to his car and drove off.

Seb helped Connie into the front seat, while Maurice got in the back. Disappointed, the onlookers drifted away.

'I didn't expect it to be this busy on a weekday,' Maurice said.

'School holidays,' Seb said briefly, as he shut the driver's side door behind him. 'What do you want? Why turn up after all these years? Why now, you bastard?'

Seb, who so rarely lost his temper, was getting angrier and angrier.

'First of all, I'm so sorry I took the baby,' Maurice said. 'He's unharmed, of course. I fed him formula and made sure he had clean nappies. I don't have much experience with babies, but I managed, and he hardly cried at all. It seemed like the only way I could talk to you both. I didn't think you would've wanted anything to do with me if I'd approached you normally.'

Seb grunted.

'As you know, Connie, your grandparents adopted me when I was about eight, as my parents and baby sister were killed in a car accident. They belonged to the same religious group. Back then, it wasn't extreme like Saul made it, though. When I was sixteen, I left home and started work. I came to see Saul occasionally... well, that isn't true. I came to see you, but I wasn't ever allowed near any of you girls. Eventually, Saul guessed I was interested in you and threatened me.'

Seb interrupted him. 'It's bloody hot sitting here. I'm going to start the engine and get the aircon working. Okay, Mum? Mum? Are you alright?'

Connie had stopped shaking but was very pale. Maurice resumed his story.

'I started running, partly because it gave me a release, partly because I thought I might see you if I went near the farm. I found I was good at it, and I met some other blokes who enjoyed it too. Before then, I'd always been a bit of a loner.'

Seb was losing patience. He was worried about his mother and itching to be with Sally and his baby. 'Get on with it,' he said tersely.

Maurice carried on as if he hadn't spoken.

'One day, I came near the farm in the early morning. I saw you riding the stallion out to the lake, so I followed you. Then I made it a routine. I just wanted to talk to you, nothing more, but I was so afraid of rejection that I couldn't speak. One morning, I ran out to the lake as normal, and there you were, talking to those guys tidying up the track. I was so angry. I couldn't talk to you, but they...'

Connie, her face set, shifted in her seat, but didn't speak. Seb opened his mouth to stop Maurice, but the words died on his lips.

'The next day – I didn't mean to hit you so hard. I was scared, and I undid your shirt to feel a pulse. Then I carried on undressing you. I knew it was wrong, but I couldn't stop. I heard someone coming and fled.' Maurice was sobbing, great dry sobs that shook the whole car.

'You bastard.' Seb looked like he would've punched Maurice if he'd been near enough. 'You raped my mother, and it nearly cost her sanity!'

Connie was crying too, and she put a hand on Seb's arm. 'Afterwards, Saul shot my horse and beat me black and blue. I wasn't allowed out for weeks. Then I found I was pregnant. Oh, God, why did you have to come back and drag it all up again?'

Seb looked at the man in the back of the car. He could see the likeness to himself. They had the same build, and although Maurice's hair was much shorter and greyer, it grew the same way. His hands, which were clutching a large handkerchief, were so like his own.

Maurice spoke again. 'I was horrified by what I'd done. I went back to the lodging house and packed up. I'd heard that someone had found you, so I wanted to get away from there as soon as I could. But I couldn't just leave like that. I slept rough for a few days, then went out to the farm, where I saw Amelia near the gate, feeding some mares. She told me what'd happened. I started to walk up the drive, and Saul appeared. I only escaped because I ran fast. One bullet tore my sleeve. I was lucky.'

They all sat quietly, busy with their own thoughts. After a while, Maurice continued.

'I'm not looking for forgiveness, or even sympathy. I know I don't deserve either. But I've been told I have advanced lung cancer, and I just wanted you to know what happened, how it happened. I'm being selfish, but I couldn't go to my grave without explaining. I've travelled the world trying to be someone else, trying to pretend I'm not a monster, but in the end I am. I'm sorry for stalking you, Connie, and for taking the baby. Many times over the last few months, I've wanted to come and speak to you, but I was convinced you wouldn't listen. Why would you? I just wanted to tell you how sorry I've always been for what I did.'

Maurice still had tears running down his face, as did Connie. Seb sat motionless. The realisation that he was sitting with his parents suddenly hit home, and everything took on an unreal aspect. For years, when he'd allowed himself to think about it, he'd wondered about his father. Connie's mother had made out he'd been an American, who Saul had murdered and buried on their farm. But nothing had ever been found, and no-one had known the truth – until now.

'I'll leave now,' Maurice said. 'I've said what I needed to say. I can't undo the past, though I wish I could. I don't deserve to be a father, let alone a grandfather.'

'How did you find us? Connie asked suddenly. 'Was it through Carmel?'

'No, I found out through my doctor in Sydney. When he told me I wasn't much longer for this world, I said I deserved to die in any case, and he asked me why. I told him I'd done a terrible thing to the only woman I'd ever loved, and that her son, who I believed was mine, was well-known in the horse world. I told him a little about you, Seb, then he said his ex-girlfriend had dated the same guy. He said it was all over before they met, but Sally was still under your spell. Then, one day, he told me you and she had reconnected. I begged him to help me find you, as before, when it all blew up in Victoria, I was abroad. In any case, the press kept your whereabouts under wraps.'

Connie made a sound between a snort and a laugh. 'That was the only decent thing they did.'

'Look, I know I've gone about this in completely the wrong way, but I was convinced you wouldn't have a bar of me if I just rang and asked to meet.'

'Too right,' Connie said, with feeling.

Mixed emotions flew around in Seb's head. He'd recognised that he resembled Maurice, though he couldn't imagine ever doing something so terrible to a woman.

'What have you done all your life?' Seb asked.

'I've worked abroad, mostly in security. I'm not working now and won't be going back. Life's too short, you know?' Maurice gave a wry smile, his eyes welling with tears, as he started to get out of the car. 'I'll disappear now. You won't be bothered by me again.'

'Wait!' Seb spoke more loudly than he'd intended, making his mother jump.

Maurice paused.

'Please wait. But first, I need to speak to Mum, alone.'

After a moment of hesitation, Maurice got out of the car. 'I'll wait over there,' he said, pointing a little distance away.

'Mum,' Seb said, 'this must be so hard for you, but – but the thing is, I'd like to speak to Maurice a little more. Would you mind?'

Connie scrunched up her sodden hankie. 'I don't know what to think, Seb. I don't remember the actual rape, but the result of it was terrible. What little freedom I had was taken away. On the other hand... it gave me you. If you want to speak to him, go ahead. It might be helpful to you. We're both revisiting a past we thought we'd left behind.'

'Thanks, Mum.' Seb leaned over and kissed his mother, then

looked back to where Maurice had been standing, only to find it empty.

Chapter 18

'He's gone!' Seb said. 'He was just over there, and now he's gone. Why didn't he wait?'

'Parked as we are, we would've seen him drive past,' Connie said.

Seb leapt out of the car and took off up the track nearest to where Maurice had been standing. Sure enough, he soon saw Maurice walking swiftly in the distance. Seb had managed to stay fairly fit, and though not dressed for running, he covered the ground quickly. He got to the lookout a few seconds after Maurice, who was leaning over the railing looking down the cliff face. For a moment, Seb froze.

'Maurice, wait!'

Maurice turned around, frowning. 'It's okay, I wasn't about to jump. I've seen it happen, and the aftermath is too horrible for those left behind.'

Seb was at a loss for words. 'Oh. Oh... good.'

'You asked me to wait, but what is it you want from me? I can't give you much. I'm pretty fucked up, as you must've realised by now.'

The two men stood regarding each other. Neither of them knew what to say. Bonded by blood but strangers by circumstance, the gulf stretched between them.

Seb mentally shook himself. He could handle damaged horses, so he should be able to manage a damaged person. It wasn't so different in some respects. As a family group came barrelling onto the platform, Seb put his hand on Maurice's shoulder and felt him flinch.

'Come, let's find a quieter spot,' Seb said.

They walked back down the track, side by side. Unconsciously, they matched their paces. Anyone looking would've recognised they were father and son. Connie, who was waiting by the information board, sucked in her breath when she saw them coming. She tried to gauge their moods. They both looked grim, but not angry.

'Mum, go home. I'm going with Maurice to where he's staying, so we can talk. It's impossible here – there are too many people.'

Maurice shot Seb a look. They hadn't agreed on that, or even talked about it. They'd walked from the lookout to the car park in silence. He realised then that Seb was used to doing things his way, and a tremor of pride shot through him. He'd been planning to disappear, but suddenly, he too wanted to spend more time with his son. *His son!*

'Okay, if you're sure,' Connie said. 'Don't be too long. Sally will be wanting you, and so will baby Joe. You haven't really had the chance to meet him yet.'

'I have a lifetime in front of me, Mum. A few more hours won't hurt.' He kissed her on the cheek. 'You okay? You look tired. Will you be alright to drive back?'

'I'll be fine, sweetheart. Just be careful. Maurice,' she acknowledged him, before getting up and walking back to her car.

Watching her go, Maurice said, 'Has she been happy?'

'Yes, she has. Come, we'll talk at your place. Where are you staying?'

'I'm renting a place out on the Rathdowney road. It's quiet there – no neighbours nearby.'

When they got to Maurice's car, Seb realised there was a lot of baby equipment on the back seat. 'Did you buy all that stuff?'

'Yes, and I read up on how to look after a small baby. It mostly worked. He's a lovely little chap, and he didn't cry that much. I don't think he liked the baby formula, though.'

'You were very determined to speak to us, but why didn't you try the normal way first?'

'Fear, uncertainty, shame. I don't know.' Maurice shuddered. 'God, what a mess I've made of my life. Connie's too.' He gripped the steering wheel tightly. 'I can't forgive myself. I loved her, you see.' Fresh tears were rolling down his face, and Seb was worried they'd have an accident.

'Let me drive, Maurice. You're in no fit state.'

They'd only just left the national park. Maurice pulled to the side, and they swapped over. Neither of them spoke again until they were on the road to Rathdowney. Seb had a sudden flashback of himself running, running down this very road. It had been night, and quite dark, but he'd managed. He'd been so hurt. Although he'd quickly realised he should've confronted his parents instead of running away, he'd convinced himself that everything would be alright if he met his grandparents. What a huge mistake that'd been. But he'd learnt from it; yes, the hard way, but he'd learnt, and it had stood him in good stead over the last few years.

He suddenly felt like telling Maurice about it. It was something he didn't like to talk about with anyone outside the family. But then, Maurice was family, in a sense.

'What do you know about me, then?' Seb asked, breaking the silence. He glanced across at Maurice, who looked pale and very tired.

'I was abroad when you were abused by Saul and only found out about it when I moved back to Sydney. The surname Windemere was in an old newspaper, and it caught my eye. I was completely horrified... then I realised I had a son. The names weren't mentioned, but soon afterwards, I came across an article about this amazing horse whisperer. There was a photo of you. It was like looking at my younger self, and the connection with horses confirmed it. The article said you were moving abroad and it was a loss to the horse world in Australia. I felt that was that. You know the rest.'

They drove in silence for a little while longer, until Maurice directed Seb onto a dirt track. It twisted and turned, then suddenly ended before a dilapidated Queenslander.

They pulled up. Although Maurice got out of the car, Seb sat still. The ticking of the cooling engine seemed amplified in the quiet.

'There's a lot you don't know,' Seb said. 'And there's a lot about you that I'd like to know.' He'd surprised himself by saying that. It hadn't been what he'd meant to say.

Maurice, who was standing by the car, looked surprised too. 'I guess that's why you insisted you come back with me.'

Seb got out of the car, and the two men went up the steps onto the rickety veranda. The house was quite small, and in need of care, but everything was very neat and tidy.

Maurice went to the fridge. 'Beer or water? I've got coffee and tea as well.'

'Water, thanks. Now I know where you live, I'd like to have a proper talk later. I need to go see Sally and meet my little son. Would you mind running me back when we've had a drink?'

Maurice shook his head, then fell into a terrible coughing fit that shook his whole frame. When he'd recovered somewhat, Seb spoke.

'How bad is the cancer?'

'Bad. This is my last hurrah, as it were. Some days I can hardly get out of bed, but I was determined to tell Connie what happened. How I was sorry, and always will be. I guessed you were stuck overseas, but I hadn't expected it would take so long for you to get here. When I heard you were coming, I was so relieved I would get to see you. I just wanted to see you. Just once.' Again, Maurice's emotions were taking over. Tears were running down his face.

'But how did you know?'

'The fruit and veg shop. Your mum gets her supplies there once a week and always has a chat. I learnt when she went, then started going in soon after and making casual remarks about how Covid's affecting people. Everyone's so consumed by it... they'd tell me about Connie and how her son was stuck abroad. Then, one day, I heard you were in quarantine in Sydney. Though I admit to spying on your family, I also read about the baby's birth in the local paper. When I realised I had a grandchild, I left a teddy bear. I saw Sally walking with him one day, it's—'

Another coughing fit took over. When Maurice finally controlled it, he looked grey and worn out. 'I need to lie down, sorry.'

'Look, I need to get back to Sally and JP. Can I take your car and bring it back tomorrow?'

Maurice nodded. 'Yes, fine.' He got to his feet and staggered out of the room. Seb sat quietly for a few moments, then got to his feet. Maurice was lying on an old swag in a room at the back of the house. His eyes were closed, his breathing shallow. Seb hovered in the doorway. 'Can I get you anything before I leave?'

Maurice shook his head. Without opening his eyes, he croaked, 'No. Just go.'

Going back into the kitchen, Seb filled a glass with water. He took it and put it on an old chair near Maurice, who didn't stir.

Seb set off for home.

At least Maurice can't disappear without a car, he thought.

Chapter 19

When he got back, the whole family was there. His sisters, nephew, niece, grandparents, brother-in-law, mother-in-law to be, his parents, Sally and his little son. At one time, gatherings of this size, even of family, would've worried him. Not now. For a time, he forgot all about Maurice, about the abduction, about everything that'd happened that day, and just enjoyed being together with his family. They all did.

Little JP was the centre of attention, but Seb didn't want anyone else to hold him. He didn't think he'd ever been more proud, or more happy. After a bit, though, JP started to cry, and not long afterwards he had terrible diarrhea. Seb and Sally were immediately very worried.

'I suspect it's the change of milk, going onto formula then back to the breast,' Connie said. 'Don't panic, you two, I'm sure he'll be okay once he's got it out of his system.'

'You look worn out,' Seb said quietly to her, later. 'Are you okay?'

She gave him a wan smile. 'I'm so glad you didn't take too long, Seb. It worried me, you going off with – with him.'

They were sitting away from everyone else, out on the veranda. He glanced round at the family, who were celebrating that Joe and Eve had returned, that the baby was unharmed, that Seb was back, that they were all together. Joan was happy; she'd been accepted into the family fold and was now relaxed and no longer fearful.

'How are you, Mum, really?'

Connie put her hand up and stroked his cheek. 'Much, much better, now you're back. We've all been so worried about you. At the moment, I feel numb about everything else. I love Sally, and I love little JP. Your Dad has been so stoic during the ups and downs we've had over the years since you were born. Again, now, too. Sorry, I'm rambling, but I'm all over the place emotionally. Somehow, I knew in my heart it was Maurice. Now you've met him, how do you feel?'

'A bit like you, really. Angry, in some respects, but I wouldn't be here if not for him. It's very strange. He's not well – I don't think he's faking that – and he's a loner. I've tended to be like that too, but Maurice is much more so than me. I think he's had a nomadic lifestyle, working round oil drilling sites. I'll take his car back tomorrow and speak with him some more. Maybe learn more. Do you mind?'

Connie shook her head. 'I still don't know how I really feel, Seb. But I do understand that he's your biological father, and now that you have the opportunity to speak with him, you should make the most of it. If you don't, I think you'll regret it. I spoke to your father about it when I got back, and he understands. You two have always been close. He doesn't feel threatened, or jealous, or hurt. So, yes, give yourself time when you take the car back. I'll come and pick you up... well, someone will. Maybe not me.'

Seb smiled. He knew there was a conflict going on inside Connie, but he also knew she would work it out herself.

That evening, when the visitors had left, Seb took Sally's hand and led her to their bedroom. Sally opened her mouth to speak, but Seb had other ideas. It was some time before they actually spoke to each other with words. Earlier in the day, they'd managed a few stolen kisses and caresses, but with a house full of people, neither of them had felt comfortable rushing off to make love. JP had also needed to be fed and looked after. Seb had tried his hand at changing his nappy, which had been a trial by fire, since JP had had diarrhea. Eventually, it had settled. Seb was already completely besotted with his baby son.

As they lay in each other's arms, Seb realised Sally was crying quietly.

'What's the matter, darling? What is it?'

Sally reached out and got a tissue from beside the bed. 'It's silly, but I'm just so happy. At times, I felt as if we would never be together again. I've never felt so low as I did the last few months. Those lockdowns knocked me for six. Our time in France was so short, it sometimes seemed like a dream – and I was so jealous of Brianna being there with you, when I couldn't be. I almost convinced myself you wouldn't love me if you ever got back home. Then there were the other women who worked for you. I worried about Marj, or whatever her name was, who kissed you.'

For a few seconds, Seb considered telling Sally about everything that'd happened with Marj, but he decided it would be best to leave it for another time.

'You and me both, Sal. Depression's dogged me these last months. It was running that saved me. If I'd still had horses around, it would've been fine, but I didn't. I really thought you and the baby would've been better off without me. As you know, I've fought demons like this before, because of Saul. I rather think Maurice has had to deal with these feelings too. I'm taking his car back tomorrow, and I was wondering if you felt like coming with JP to pick me up. I know it's a big ask, but what do you think?'

'I didn't feel threatened by him, so yes, I'll do that.'

Shortly after, JP decided he wanted attention, and between one thing and another, not much sleep was had that night.

The next morning, it was a slow start for everyone, except Alec. He had several machines to see to.

'Why does everyone want everything done before Christmas?' he said to Connie, as he rushed out the door. 'It's not some sort of milestone that we'll all stop working after.'

Connie smiled to herself. Then Seb appeared, followed by Sally, who was carrying JP. They had a glow of happiness about them, which was good to see, especially after all the ups and downs of recent days.

'I'm taking Maurice's car back, and Sally's going to pick me up. Then we thought we might go to the real estate office in town and see what's about. I'd like something similar to Granny and Grandpa's place, though with more land, as they only have the one paddock.'

Connie gave Seb a quick hug.

'I'm going over to theirs later, as I haven't ridden for a day or so, and my horse will wonder what I've been up to. You must come and see him, Seb and tell me what you think.'

'Of course – you bought him after I'd left for England. Yes, I will. Maybe later this arvo.'

Connie gave a small chuckle. 'You're back using Aussie expressions already!'

Seb grinned. 'Sure am, sure am.'

After he'd gone, Sally sat down at the table. 'Connie, can I ask you something, please?'

'Yes, what is it? Is it about Maurice?'

'How do you really feel about him?'

'Angry. Very angry. I don't think I'll ever forgive him for what he did. But a long time ago, I learnt that anger doesn't heal. If I lived the rest of my life feeling angry, I would be eaten up inside. So, I'm trying to accept what has gone before and simply move on.'

'Oh, Connie, you're such a strong, brave woman. Thank you. This has been very helpful.' Sally kissed Connie and hugged her tightly.

***

It was a glorious day, with a breeze stopping it from being too hot. Seb decided he liked the road out to Rathdowney. It was varied, with hills and valleys, farms and bushland. As he turned onto Maurice's rental property, he noticed that the bush was encroaching upon it in places. What had once been a garden in front of the old house was very overgrown and neglected. There were some roses struggling to survive, and a long-dead vine covered one end of the veranda. Looking closely, Seb saw that a few boards were missing from the house. It would take more than a coat of paint to make it look presentable; even the roof looked as if it had rusted through in places.

Although it wasn't a big house, it must've once been very beautiful. Above the door, there was a lovely stained-glass window, and the doorframe was carved. He called out as he mounted the steps. No reply. He called again and heard an answer from the back of the house. Maurice was sitting in an old cane chair in the lounge. He looked grey and exhausted, and very thin.

'Hey, Maurice. I've brought morning tea – stopped at the bakery in town. I hope you like pastries.'

Maurice's eyes filled with sudden tears, and he turned his head away.

'I'll make coffee or tea,' Seb said. 'Which would you like?'

Maurice found that he had to struggle to his feet, partly because the old chair was very low, and partly because he was feeling weak, not like himself at all.

'Thanks, but it's okay. I'll do it. I know where everything is.'

A few minutes later, they were seated again, with a pastry and a steaming cup of coffee each.

'How are Sally and my little grandson? Tell me about your dad. He seems a good bloke.'

'He is. I've been so lucky. We were, and still are, very, very close. I was so silly when I ran away. I didn't even stop to ask questions. But then, if I had, I wouldn't have met Sally, or found out how important horses are to me.'

'You had a bad time in Victoria, didn't you?'

Seb gave Maurice a potted version of what had happened before, then asked him about himself.

'Well, after I fled from Saul, I bummed around for a while. Got odd jobs down in Melbourne. Slept rough for a time, then joined the army and got kicked out for misbehaving. Long story. Not worth repeating. Then I started working for a security company that looks after oil wells in dangerous places. So that's my life in a nutshell; I've been to extraordinary places and seen quite a lot of the world. With my record, women have been off my radar. I didn't trust myself.'

With Seb's prompting, Maurice related some of the places he'd been and things he'd seen. Not all of them good.

'Tell me about your horses and how you train them,' Maurice said, afterwards.

'To be completely honest, I'm not even sure how it works. Horses just seem to instinctively trust me. I'm always calm, and always speak softly, even if I feel like raising my voice. I'll get back into it as soon as I can find the right property. Have to get Christmas over with too, as nothing much happens then, businesswise.'

Seb saw a shadow pass across Maurice's face and could've kicked himself. Christmas couldn't be much fun for someone in his shoes.

Just then, he heard a car. He said, with some relief, 'That may be Sally. She was going to pick me up.' He got to his feet.

Maurice stayed where he was. 'I won't come out. She won't want to see me.'

However, just then, they heard a 'Cooee, Seb? Are you there?' and Sally came through the house, carrying the baby.

Maurice stumbled to his feet, looking aghast.

'Hello, Maurice,' Sally said. 'I thought you might like to see JP again. He's wide awake, so this is your chance. He sleeps a lot. Connie said I'm lucky – lots of babies don't.'

Tears were trickling down Maurice's face again.

'I never expected this,' he croaked. 'Sally, how can you forgive me?'

Sally put her head to one side. 'I haven't. I still feel very angry, but anger doesn't help anyone. Seb tells me you're not long for this earth, so maybe that makes it easier. If JP had come to any harm, we'd be talking to the police.'

Turning, she got a chair out of the kitchen and sat down.

'Interesting old house, this,' she remarked. 'I bet it could tell a tale. The buildings in Bergerac where wonderful, weren't they, Seb?'

'Yes, though I stopped looking after seeing you again.'

Maurice looked up from watching his grandson. 'Tell me about it. I never got to France.'

So, the talk turned to how they'd met again. JP yawned and shut his eyes, and they all laughed. Sally and Seb hadn't heard Maurice laugh before, and it was deep and happy, but also sounded as if he didn't do it often.

'We have to go,' Seb said. 'The family will be having lunch soon. What are your plans now, Maurice?'

'The rent's paid until the end of the month. It'll take me a while to pack up, as I never intended to be here this long. Somehow, I seem to have gathered stuff.'

Maurice accompanied them out to the car. As Sally was putting the baby in the car seat, Seb stood looking around. 'Is there much land?' He could see the remains of old buildings far to the right of the house.

'I've explored a bit. There's a large dam behind those buildings, which is where the house's water comes from. I believe there are about twenty hectares altogether. It belongs to the people who live in that big house before the turn-in to this place. It was all one property when they bought it, but they didn't want this part, so they put it up for sale. Seems no-one's bitten, though. I heard about it in the pub one evening after I first arrived.'

'You stopped when my car was playing up, to see if I needed help,' Sally said.

'Yes, I did, as I didn't have an address for Seb's family. Christopher, who told me about you coming to visit, suggested that I follow you. So, I have to confess I did. Though I only caught up with you on the approach to Tamworth, and that was by sheer luck.'

'But how did you know it was me?'

'I saw you and Chris having dinner together before you left. Again, it was just luck. I saw him and was about to say hello when something stopped me. I guessed who you were, and as you'd driven to meet him, I saw your car. The rest was easy.'

Sally shivered. 'That was creepy. And you've been watching us, haven't you? Me and Connie and everyone.' With that, she got into the car. She was looking angry again.

'Sorry.' Maurice turned away.

Seb stood watching him go towards the house. He couldn't leave it like this.

'Just a minute, Sal.'

He ran and caught up with Maurice. 'I'll come again before you leave.'

Maurice looked at Seb with dark eyes, so like his own. They were full of pain. 'I only seem to be good at stuffing things up. But if you really want to, that's fine by me.'

With that, he climbed the steps to the veranda. Seb returned to the car and drove them home.

Chapter 20

Over the next two days, Sally and Seb really caught up with each other, and Seb found he couldn't get enough of his little son either. He could hardly let JP or Sally out of his sight. Making love to Sally was another top priority, until one morning, Sally said, 'I'll get pregnant again, at this rate.'

They'd just made love. Seb's eyes, which had been half-closed, flew open. 'I thought it was unlikely for you to get pregnant when you're breastfeeding?'

'It still happens, Seb. But don't worry – we'll go with the flow. In any case, I don't want to wait too long to give JP a brother or sister.'

Seb watched her get out of bed and head for the shower. A few minutes later, JP woke up.

'You know what, little mate,' Seb said, as he picked him up, 'your daddy really needs to find a place for us to live. Especially if your mummy gets pregnant again soon. Trouble is, Christmas is only ten days away now. Your first Christmas! What do you think?'

Sally came back, wrapped in a towel.

'This little guy wants his breakfast,' Seb said. 'Sal, I need to look for somewhere for us to live. I know I haven't been here long, but everything comes to a stop around Christmas and New Year, so I want to spend the next day or so seeing what I can find. Do you mind? I'll go and look, and if I think anything's a possibility, I'll come and get you. I don't think we want to drag JP round looking at places in the heat.'

Sally agreed, so later that morning, Seb set off. By the afternoon, he was feeling deflated. He'd looked at three places, but none of them had been right. The last one was on the Rathdowney road. Seb was about to drive past the place Maurice was renting, when on the spur of the moment, he swung into the track leading to the house.

Everything looked much the same, except that Maurice's car was at the front of the house, and it was plain he was packing up.

Seb went into the house. There was no sign of Maurice anywhere. Seb called out but received no reply. For the first time, he took in his surroundings. It wasn't a big house, but at some point, it had been cared for. With its polished wooden floors, and the stained-glass panes in some windows and above the front door, it must've been a lovely house in the past.

However, Seb wanted to find Maurice now he was there. He went out the back and looked at the other buildings, which were in a state of decay. No Maurice. A path led into the bush behind the buildings, so Seb followed it. It twisted and turned, until suddenly, he came out of the trees into a large, cleared area. In the middle was a big dam. Sitting on the bank, with his back to Seb, was Maurice. The scene was picturesque, with its backdrop of mountains, trees, and water, and the large paddock, though overgrown, was beautiful. Seb approached Maurice.

He turned. Seb almost stopped walking, horrified by the look of utter despair and misery on his face. He covered it up with a small smile, but it didn't reach his eyes.

'Hello. Didn't expect to see you.'

Seb grinned. 'Well, I was passing by, so I thought I'd drop in.'

'Are you alone?' Maurice looked behind Seb, back towards the house.

'Yep. Been looking for a property, without much luck.'

'What sort of money are we talking about? I'm guessing if you want it for horses, you'll have to spend a bit. They say prices have risen since this pandemic kicked off.'

Seb sat down near him. 'I'm lucky – I sold my place in the UK for silly money. I was able to pay off the mortgage, and with the exchange rate in my favour, I'm hoping to buy a place outright.'

Maurice raised his eyebrows and looked at his son with new respect. 'You've done well. Is it hard, training or retraining these horses? I've followed you in the press since I found out about you, though everything seems at a distance. You don't ever give interviews.'

'No way! It was hard enough when everything blew up in Victoria. Poor Mum. She's so strong… I don't know how she got through it all.'

They sat in silence for a bit. It was a comfortable quiet, though, each busy with their own thoughts. Then, Maurice said, 'Why don't you buy this place? It wants a lot spent on it, but it's a great location, and the house could be lovely if it was renovated.'

Seb looked at him, surprised. It hadn't even occurred to him. It was a beautiful spot where they were – a large paddock surrounded by trees, with the mountains in the background.

'How large is it? Do you know?'

Maurice shook his head. 'Not sure. About a hundred hectares, I think. There's a smaller paddock over there, as well as the one near the house. That was sectioned off at some point. If you look, you can see the remains of fencing.'

Seb got to his feet. 'Come on, walk round with me. This is very interesting. You might've come up with a good idea.'

They fought their way across the paddock. The grass, though dead, was pretty tangled. Both watched out for snakes but didn't see any. On the far side, they came to the remains of an old fence.

The posts were still there, and in places, the wire was showing, though it was knotted with the grass and bushes. A patch of lantana took up quite a large area. They turned right when they got to the corner. Then, at Maurice's suggestion, they retraced their steps until they came to the corner post on the other side.

'How big do you reckon this paddock is, Maurice?' Seb asked, as he stood looking around.

'It's got to be at least sixty acres, and it's reasonably flat. There's just a small slope over that side. I assume flat is better?'

'It's not, necessarily. Only for a training ground, and there's plenty of room by the buildings, I think.'

Seb's mind was in overdrive. He was feeling optimistic and excited. When they got back to the house, he explored what remained of the buildings. The barn was in quite good order, but when he stepped inside, he had a flashback to the barn in Victoria and stopped so suddenly that Maurice ran into him. Seb stood still and tried to get his racing heart back to its normal rate.

'What's wrong?' Maurice asked.

'Nothing. Actually, I'm not going in there. Bad memories.'

He turned and walked back towards the house. Maurice frowned but had the sense not to ask questions.

Seb reached his car. 'I'd better go. Sally will be wondering where I am.'

Before Maurice could answer, he got in and drove off.

Maurice stood watching the car disappear. He sighed. It had all been going so well, but he didn't know if he would see Seb again, as he was planning on leaving the following day. The depression that had been sitting on his shoulder when Seb turned up enveloped him again. A coughing fit racked his body, and he staggered indoors to get a drink of water.

What did I expect? he asked himself. As it was, he'd already received far more than he'd ever anticipated. The plan had been to see Connie and Seb and explain what he'd done. He wasn't looking for any kind of forgiveness; he just wanted to clear his mind before it was too late. The doctors had told him he'd had a year left at most, which was up in January. He knew he was on borrowed time, but somehow, coming up here and planning his encounter with Connie and Seb seemed to have helped put his illness on hold. Now, it was back, and doing anything was hard.

Seb breathed deeply as he drove away. God, how pathetic he'd been. Emotion had caught him by surprise, and he'd almost panicked.

He slowed down as he neared home. He'd hardly said goodbye, and he thought Maurice may be leaving the next day. Against his will, he'd found a connection with Maurice that he'd neither expected nor wanted – but he couldn't deny it was there.

'Are you alright, Seb?' his mother asked as he came into the kitchen. 'Sal's feeding Joe.'

To her surprise, he came up and hugged her tight.

'Love you, Mum.'

'What's brought that on?'

'I'll tell you later,' Seb said, then went in search of Sally.

When he walked into the bedroom, Sally, who was sitting on the edge of the bed breastfeeding JP, could also tell something had upset him. 'What's wrong?'

'God, I must be very transparent. Mum asked the same question.'

'We love you, so we can see when something's up. That's all.'

'It's so silly, and I feel pathetic now, but I popped in to see Maurice on my way back and end up looking round the property. It's big, and I reckon it may suit us. The house needs renovation, but the land is ideal.'

'Okay. Then why do you look as if you've seen a ghost?'

'We started to look at the buildings... the only one not in a bad state is the barn, and I had the most horrible flashback to the barn down in Victoria. It was as if I were there again. It's so silly. I haven't had that happen for a long time.'

He sat beside Sally. She put her free arm round him, and he buried his head in her neck.

'I expect it's because you've seen Maurice, and all these old memories have come to the surface,' she said. 'The place sounds exciting, though, even if the barn's a worry. Can I come with you to look?'

'Of course. We'll go first thing. I think Maurice is leaving tomorrow, but I'd like to see him before he goes.'

'Mm. Well, I can live with that, especially if he's going.'

'Sorry, Sal. He looks bad – he was pretty puffed just walking across flat ground. I don't know how long he's got left.'

Chapter 21

The next morning, Seb and Sally set off in good time, as Seb was a little worried Maurice would leave before they got there. *If that's the case,* he thought, *so be it.*

When they reached the house, Seb was surprised by how pleased he was to see that Maurice's car was still there. There was a large suitcase sitting beside it, but no sign of Maurice himself. While Sally got JP out of his car seat, Seb went to the door and called out. He heard a small sound coming from the bedroom. Maurice was on top of the swag, sweating profusely and struggling to breathe. Seb's first thought was of the virus, but where would Maurice have got it from? He pulled out his phone to call the paramedics.

'No, don't, please,' Maurice rasped. 'I'll be alright soon. My inhaler's in the kitchen, and I couldn't quite make it.'

Sally had appeared, carrying JP in a sling. Upon hearing what Maurice said, she went and got the inhaler.

Maurice sat up and took a few puffs. 'I'll be okay. Did too much too quickly, that's all.'

Sally went to the kitchen and bustled about making coffee, while Seb helped Maurice up. Keeping a hold on his elbow, Seb walked him into the kitchen. Sally looked round and was struck again by how alike they looked.

Maurice sank down at the table and took the mug of coffee

Sally held out. 'Thank you, love,' he said gruffly. Sally and Seb exchanged looks. Maurice really wasn't well, though he hid it most of the time.

'I wanted to show Sal round, if that's okay?'

'It's not my place, so do as you like,' Maurice said. 'I was going to leave an hour or so ago, but I'll sit here for a bit, I think.'

'Please don't leave yet,' Seb said. 'You don't look fit to drive.'

'It's time I went, before I do something else stupid.'

'Maurice,' Sally said, 'I don't think you should go anywhere until you're feeling better. I can't forgive you, but I don't like seeing you suffer either.'

Tears gathered in Maurice's eyes. He gulped. 'That means a lot, what you've just said. I don't deserve it.'

Sally came across and put her hand on his arm. 'I never felt threatened when I saw you the other times.'

'Thanks, Sally,' Maurice said, touching her hand lightly. 'My son is a lucky man.'

Now the tears spilled over; Seb too was caught up in the emotion.

Sally took charge. 'Now, no going anywhere until we return. We won't be trudging across the paddock Seb described. We'll just go as far as the dam, then maybe look round this part near the house.'

She raised her eyebrows at Seb. He grinned. 'You're the boss.'

Without further ado, they set off. The path to the dam was well-worn, so it was easy walking.

'Oh, wow, I can see why you like this,' Sally said, when they got to the dam and paused to look around. 'It's sheltered and secluded, and the view's stunning. I love it!'

'The boundary fence is just beyond that tree line over there. It'll all need replacing, but it's quite doable.'

After a time, they retraced their steps back to the buildings. JP had been asleep, but now he opened his eyes and gave an enormous yawn.

'Do you want to feed him now?' Seb asked. 'We can do this later.'

Sally took a long, hard look at him. 'Delaying tactics? Come on – the sooner we lay your ghosts to rest, the better.'

Seb sighed inwardly. It had been a delaying tactic. As the other buildings were ruined, the barn was the only one they could enter.

Sally marched ahead of him and went in through what had once been big double doors. Seb followed reluctantly, keeping his eyes on her back. There was an old tractor siting in the middle, and the remains of some old hay bales in one corner. Otherwise, apart from cobwebs and grime, the barn was empty.

'I don't know an awful lot about these things, but it looks in good nick to me,' Sally said, being as practical and down-to-earth as she could. 'You could put stables in here. Enough to house quite a few horses.'

'No!' Seb's voice came out harsher than he'd meant it to. 'We'll use this for storage, or maybe as a small training area. The barn in Victoria was American-style, like this, with stables on either side and a passage down the middle. I'm not going to replicate it.'

'Seb, darling, maybe that's exactly what you should do. If we make it a happy place, it might erase those bad memories forever. It would be different, anyway – it's a different setting, and the design would be different. We could change all sorts of little things.'

Seb stared at her for several seconds. Sally, thinking she'd gone too far, opened her mouth to speak. Then Seb said, 'I'm the luckiest man alive, to be with a wise woman like you. I love you so much, Sal.' He put his arms around her, and little JP in the sling, and kissed her thoroughly.

Soon after, they made their way back towards the house, but Seb stopped abruptly before they reached it. 'Tomorrow, we'll go to Brisbane to get you a ring. Then we'll start planning our wedding. That's most important. Afterwards, we'll see if we can buy this place – we have to remember it's not actually on the market.'

'Well, why don't we go and see the owners after we've finished here?'

Seb grinned at her. 'I can see why you were so good at your job.'

When they entered the house, they found Maurice asleep, slumped at the kitchen table with his head on his arms. He roused as they came in. JP, who wanted feeding, started to cry. Sally sat down at the table and, turning her back to Maurice, put JP to her breast.

Seb was soon enthusing to Maurice about his plans for the barn and the place as a whole. Maurice sat nodding, not saying much. Realising he looked sad, Seb ran out of steam.

'I'm sorry, going on like that was insensitive of me. How are you feeling?'

'Better than an hour ago, thanks. I really need to get going. I've packed everything up, so it's time to leave.'

'What happens at Christmas, Maurice?' Sally asked.

A shadow passed across his face. 'It's just a day. I don't do anything different.'

'There's no-one in Sydney who you could spend it with?' Seb asked.

'This is only the second Christmas I won't be on some drilling site overseas. I don't have anyone in Sydney. In fact, you guys are my only known relatives.'

Seb and Sally exchanged a look. Maurice got to his feet.

'Well, this is it. I must away.' He patted his pocket. 'I've got my medication at hand if I need it. Don't know how far I'll get today, as it's later than I thought I'd leave.'

'Why not put it off until tomorrow?' Sally asked.

'Never put off till tomorrow what you can do today, as I was always told. No, it's better I go now, before – before I get used to seeing you.' He swallowed hard, then moved towards the door.

'Wait!' Seb exclaimed, but Maurice kept going as if he hadn't heard. Seb went after him. 'Wait,' he said again, as he caught up. Maurice turned and patted him on the shoulder. Then, without speaking, he opened his car door. Seb went to catch hold of it, but Maurice was too quick for him. He started the car and drove off. Seb stood watching him go, aware that he was too emotional to stop or to speak. Seb knew what that was like.

Sally appeared, with JP still attached to her breast. 'He's gone, then. But what about the house? Has he paid the rent up to date? I know he was camping, but there's tea, coffee, milk and bread in the kitchen. He'd packed his swag – must've done that while we were looking round. What about locking up?' Then she saw Seb's face. 'Oh, darling. You're upset.'

Seb shook his head. 'This is all so stupid. This strange man waltzes into our lives and pretty much upsets us all. Then, just as we get to know him a little, he ups and disappears again. I don't like the thought of him alone at Christmas, or alone with his illness. He's my father, for good or bad. I don't want it to be like this. Marj lost her brother to Covid – they'd quarrelled years ago and not made up. She thought she had time, but then he was dead, and I've never seen anyone more upset than she was. I want a bit more time with Maurice. He's dying, and time is short. Why did he go like that?'

'He's still punishing himself for what he did to Connie. Perhaps he always will. Look, we better go and see the owners of this place. After that, we'll make a plan.'

'What do you mean?'

'Well, by Maurice's state, I don't think he'll drive far tonight. Maybe we can track him down tomorrow.'

'But we won't know which way he's gone.'

'That's true, but I also think you need to talk to Alec and Connie if you're going to persuade him to hang around a bit longer.'

Seb knew Sally was right. After clearing up a few things, they found there were no keys or locks anywhere. In the end, they just drove to the owners' house, to tell them Maurice had left and sound them out about buying the property.

They'd half-expected to find an older couple, but were met by a young pair, Jenny and Paul, whom they hit it off with immediately.

'We bought the whole place seven years ago,' Paul said. 'The old house across the road was the main part of the property, but we liked this side better. However, my business took a dive, and once we'd built this place, we couldn't afford to do anything about the land across the road. We'd be happy to sell it to you at the right price.'

'How much were you thinking?' Seb asked. 'Even the land's in a bad way. It needs a shedload of money spent on it.'

They were sitting on a big deck at the back of the house, with cold drinks in front of them. Paul scratched his head. 'Give me a day to think it through, and I'll call you.' He paused, looking at Seb keenly. 'Was he some relation of yours, that guy? There's a likeness.'

Seb mentally wriggled, then said, 'My estranged father, actually. I only met him a few days ago.'

Seeing he was going to be asked more questions, he hurriedly changed the topic.

Chapter 22

When they returned home, Seb called Alec up from the workshop and sat him and Connie at the kitchen table. He then told them about Maurice.

'What are you wanting us to say, Seb?' Connie asked. 'Are you suggesting he stays here and spends Christmas with us? In any case, he's already left.'

'No, I was just going to say that if he came back and stayed where he was, we – Sally and I – could visit him on Christmas Day at least.'

'I'm not sure about this,' Connie said. 'I can't forgive him.'

Alec leant across the table and took her hand, giving it a soft, reassuring squeeze.

'I know, Mum,' Seb said. 'You don't have to, and I haven't either. I just don't like to think of him being alone on Christmas.'

Connie nodded. 'Alright, then. I understand.'

'I'll try his mobile,' Seb said. 'I got him to give me his number the other day. We don't know which way he was travelling.'

A few minutes later, Seb sighed in frustration. 'His phone's either switched off or has no reception. It just goes to voicemail.'

'Try later,' Connie said.

'The other thing is, Sal and I want to go to Brisbane to get a ring.'

'Seb, darling,' Sally said, 'it'll be hellish this close to Christmas. I can wait a little longer for a ring. I'm here with you, and I really don't fancy fighting the hordes of shoppers. I don't feel like leaving JP either just now.'

'Sally's right,' Connie said. 'It'll be very busy, and you don't like crowds either.'

By bedtime, Seb was still frustrated, as Maurice's phone continued to ring out.

'We could drive to Warwick tomorrow, if you want,' Sally suggested.

'Trouble is, he could've gone any number of ways. I'll try again in the morning. Right now, I have more pressing needs,' he said, taking Sally into his arms and kissing her. All thoughts of Maurice fled their minds.

***

Water, water in his mouth, in his ears and eyes. He was sinking. He couldn't fight it. His hands were bound, and everything was dark.

'Seb! Seb, wake up! You're having a nightmare.'

Sally shook him awake. For a few minutes, he lay staring at her. 'Oh, God, that was a bad one.'

'It's okay, I'm here. It's gone now. I was actually feeding JP and was pleased you hadn't woken, though it might've been better if you had.'

She wrapped her arms around him and was asleep again very quickly.

Seb lay looking at the ceiling. He'd had nightmares on and off ever since that fateful time in Victoria, though this one was really lingering – usually, once he was awake, he could shake them off.

His mind turned to Maurice. Why wasn't he answering his phone? Was it because he didn't want any more contact? The thoughts went round and round in Seb's head.

***

Maurice hadn't gone far. He felt too unwell and had needed to stop. But he'd recognised that he was getting fond of Sally, and that he loved his son. It was all very confusing. He'd never been close to anyone all his life – had never allowed himself to be, ever since what he'd done to Connie. His shame was like his cancer. It had eaten away at him, so at times he'd been little more than an empty shell, just going through the motions expected of him, finding it hard at times to empathise with any other human. Now, suddenly, that had all changed. He'd wanted to see his son but hadn't expected it would have such an effect on him. He knew he loved Seb. Who would've thought he could experience this overpowering feeling? He was so proud of the man Seb was – kind, thoughtful and magic with horses. He would've liked to have seen that skill.

Maurice sat in his car. He'd driven as far as Lake Maroon, thinking of going to Rathdowney and heading south. However, he'd found he hadn't been able to concentrate on driving very well, so he'd stopped before he had an accident. He'd hurt enough people in his life.

He'd parked so he was looking at the lake. It was beautiful. The day was getting hot, so he got out of the car and sat down at an empty picnic spot.

He woke with a start. It was cool now, and the sun was going down. Uncomfortable though he was, he'd slept for a long time. He felt a few hunger pains. He'd only had a slice of toast for breakfast and hadn't packed any food. He was very stiff and felt light-headed. Shuffling over to the car, he found a bottle of water and a couple of stale biscuits. They didn't seem to make much difference to how he was feeling.

Time passed, but he couldn't rouse himself to move again from the picnic bench. It all seemed such an effort. He dozed, on and off. Then, at last, he managed to think clearly and decided to get back on the road. He'd make good progress this time of night, with little traffic. He felt grimy, so he scrambled down the steep bank to the water's edge. Squatting, he cupped his hands, scooped some water up and rubbed his face. It didn't seem to help much, so he leant further forward – and, to his horror, lost his balance.

He fell face-first into the lake. It was a shock. The water was cold, and the bottom was muddy. Water was up his nose, in his eyes and mouth, and his feet were stuck to the bottom. He managed to turn himself over and, after a lot of struggling, got himself back onto the bank. It felt as if a tight band were around his chest, and breathing was difficult. He lapsed into unconsciousness.

He was aware of voices, but he couldn't make out what they were saying. It was all too hard. He opened his eyes slightly, but all he could make out were blurry faces looking at him, with a bright light behind.

Closing his eyes again, he allowed himself to drift away.

***

Seb and Sally were the last to emerge for breakfast, and only Connie was in the kitchen.

'Do you two want a cooked breakfast?' she asked. 'I'll make one if you do. Otherwise, help yourselves.'

'Thanks, Mum. I'll just have toast,' said Seb.

Sally nodded. 'Same for me.'

Connie smiled. 'Seb, I've noticed you haven't changed your eating habits from when you were running.'

'No, I haven't.' He paused. 'I'm just going to try Maurice one more time. If I can't get hold of him, I suppose that's that. He obviously doesn't want to hear from me.' As he said it, he felt a small stab of hurt, which surprised him.

Connie saw the emotion cross his face. She understood that they'd made a tentative friendship and was surprised to find she didn't mind. She wondered how Alec felt. She'd ask him when she got the chance. How did he really feel about Seb spending time with Maurice? After all, he and Seb had always been very close.

As Seb got up from the table, they heard a car draw up outside. He went to the door, opening it just as a policeman was stretching out his hand to ring the bell.

'Hello, something wrong?'

'Well...'

Another officer joined the first. Seb glanced from one to the other. This looked serious.

He stood back. 'You'd better come in.'

They followed Seb into the kitchen, and Connie and Sally looked up in alarm. 'What is it, Seb?' Sally asked.

He shrugged. The first policeman said, 'Nothing to concern you folks. A man was found unconscious at Lake Maroon. He'd been there overnight, which was against the rules. We think he must've fallen in at some stage, as he was muddy and wet. He was found at first light this morning. His driver's licence and other paperwork were in the car, along with your address, though there was no name.'

'Is he dead?' Seb asked.

'No. Sir, do you know this person?'

Connie spoke up. 'We all do and were concerned for him.

Where is he?'

'He was in Boonah, to start with, but they transferred him to Ipswich.' The officer looked keenly at Seb. 'Is he a relation?' He'd seen the man in the ambulance and thought there was a similarity.

'No... yes, sort of.' Seb was thrown into confusion.

'I see, sir,' the officer said, though he plainly didn't.

Connie spoke up. 'What about his car and belongings?'

'The car's still there. Someone needs to remove it, or it'll have to go into the pound in Ipswich.'

Connie and Seb exchanged a look, then Alec came striding into the kitchen. He'd seen the police car and was worried something was amiss. 'What's happened?'

'It's Maurice,' Connie said. 'He's taken ill and is in Ipswich hospital.'

'Dad, could you run me out to Lake Maroon?' Seb asked. 'Then I could at least bring his car back. Also, we need to find out how bad he is. Do you know?' He turned to the police officers.

'The paramedics thought he was severely dehydrated and cold, though I also heard him say he has cancer, which wouldn't have helped.'

Connie went to the phone. 'One way to find out,' she said, taking it into the office.

'Tea or coffee?' Alec asked the policemen.

'Neither, thank you, sir. We just have to go over a few formalities, then we'll leave you in peace.'

Five minutes later, they left, after asking a few questions. Seb, who'd become spokesman, had parried them as best he could. They may have asked more but were called away to something more urgent.

Connie came back. 'The receptionist at the hospital wasn't too keen to speak to me, until I told them I was related to Maurice. Legally, he is my step-uncle, though that's stretching it a bit. Anyway, he was dehydrated, hypothermic and of course not well anyway. They think he muddled his drugs up, or at least didn't take them as he should. He'd told them he had no-one to be discharged to. They were going to keep him in, but now that I've talked to them, they seem keen to allow him out. I said someone would pick him up later today. I hope I've done the right thing.'

'What right thing?'

Joe had just come into the kitchen. He and Eve had been busy since they got home, settling back into their house. Connie explained what had happened.

'He could stay in our van,' Joe said. 'It's by the house and easy enough to connect to the mains. That way, we can keep an eye on him until he's stronger, at least over Christmas. I'll ring Eve now and tell her what's happening, then I'll go and collect him.'

'You haven't met him before, Joe,' Connie said. 'I'm not sure how he'll be. I could come with you, I suppose.' She looked apprehensive but determined.

So, it was all organised. Alec and Seb went off to retrieve Maurice's car; the police had locked it but given the key to Seb. He gave Sally a kiss and said they would be back soon. Joe and Connie left too, and suddenly, Sally found herself alone with the baby. She sat at the kitchen table, feeding him, and a feeling of contentment swept over her.

I'm so lucky, she thought. *I'm with the love of my life, I have a beautiful son, and we're about to have our own place. At the same time, I'm part of an amazing family that is forgiving and kind, and it'll be Christmas in a few days. Many all over the world are suffering with this horrible virus... this last little while, I'd almost forgotten about it, but soon they'll start vaccinating, and everything will be back to normal.*

Little did Sally know, there was a very, very long road ahead before that was going to even start to happen.

Chapter 23

Collecting the car was easy, and it wasn't long before Alec and Seb were back. Sally, who'd been tidying the kitchen, put her arms around Seb and told him her happy thoughts. A light kiss turned into a passionate one, and a few minutes later, they were back in the bedroom, urgently making love. Somehow, it was very erotic. It was the middle of the morning, with people not far away, and both knew there were other things they could've been doing.

Seb, spent, stroked Sally's face. 'God, woman, I didn't expect that. You're amazing. Let's just get married as soon as we can organise a celebrant. I don't want a fuss; I'd like to creep off, only you and me, but that would hurt the family, especially Mum. Let's have a small ceremony as soon as we can. What do you say?'

'I can't wait either, Seb. Let's do it. I always knew we wouldn't have a big wedding, as crowds aren't your thing, in any case. But we can't before Christmas – it's only three days away.'

'I keep forgetting that. So much has happened, this last week.' Seb started to get dressed. 'Better get busy! There's lots to do.'

***

When Connie and Joe reached the hospital, they had to go through all the normal formalities before they finally got to see Maurice. He was sitting on the side of a bed, wearing a hospital gown, his clothes in a bag beside him. Joe had brought a shirt and shorts of his, as they'd known Maurice's clothes would be in a state.

Connie thought that Maurice looked a very old man, just then. He was haggard and frail, and when he saw Connie, his eyes filled with tears.

'Didn't expect to see you, Connie,' he croaked.

'We've come to collect you. This is Joe, my father-in-law.' Connie indicated Joe, who was standing behind her. They'd talked about Maurice, and how she felt about him, on the way to the hospital. Joe immediately saw the likeness to Seb.

'Here. These may not fit, but they'll get you back.' Joe passed over his clothes. 'We'll wait outside while you get dressed.'

A few minutes later, they made their way to the car. Maurice still seemed a little unsteady on his feet but declined the offer of Joe's arm. The clothes hung off him, and Connie was shocked by how thin he was. She hadn't noticed it before but also guessed he was losing weight rapidly.

'You sit in the front, Maurice,' said Joe.

Both Connie and Maurice found it surreal sitting next to each other in the car, though neither of them mentioned it. At first, no-one in the car spoke. Then, Maurice said, 'Are you dropping me back at my car or the house I was living in?'

'Neither,' said Joe. 'We're going to my place. You can stay in the caravan, at least until Christmas is over.'

'But—'

'No buts. Rightly or wrongly, you're Seb's natural father. He is my much-loved grandson, so I'm doing this for him. If Connie can put up with you, then so can the rest of us. Right?'

Maurice's throat closed. He nodded, overwhelmed by their generosity. All his life, he'd been unemotional, except for just after he'd raped Connie. People had always thought him a cold fish. Now, his feelings were raw and uncontrollable. All those years of self-hatred had given way to a flood of tears and thankfulness for what these people were doing for him. He knew he didn't deserve it, but he wouldn't throw it back in their faces.

Connie started to point out landmarks, as she thought it best to distract Maurice. It worked, and they talked like tourists all the rest of the way back. As they drew into Joe's place, they saw Maurice's car sitting by the caravan. Seb had heard them draw up and was soon by the car, opening Maurice's door. He put his hand under Maurice's elbow and helped him to his feet. Then, without forethought, he hugged his father.

Maurice couldn't have been more taken aback. He couldn't ever remember being hugged before, and again, tears trickled down his face.

'Seb, son,' he croaked. Seb had tears in his eyes too. Then Eve came bustling out.

'Come in, Maurice, and have a coffee or tea – or maybe a cold drink. It's a scorcher today, isn't it?' No-one had really noticed.

'Seb and I will head home now,' Connie said. She was worried about all she had to do to get ready for Christmas, and the emotionally-charged atmosphere was getting to her a bit.

A few moments, later she and Seb were on their way home.

'You alright, Mum?'

'Yes, funnily enough. What haunted me just as much as the rape was all that went after – Saul's cruelty in blaming me and poor Jasper. He was a very special horse, and the stud wasn't the same afterwards. It was the start of the decline.'

'He was one very screwed-up man, wasn't he?'

'He did such evil things,' Connie said with contemplation.

'I don't think he was ever happy, though when I was small, I don't remember it being quite so bad. Maybe that's my memory playing tricks. He certainly turned Mum into a madwoman too.' She took a deep breath. 'Come on, Christmas is here, and we have so much to do. We haven't even decorated the tree yet, and it's been sitting there waiting nearly a week!'

Seb laughed. 'I'm sure it doesn't mind. Mum, Sally and I want to tie the knot as quickly as possible, only in front of immediate family. We don't want anything big. Just a quiet ceremony, and a nice meal afterwards.'

Connie was silent for a moment. 'Are you sure Sally's happy with that? Most women want to push the boat out, especially when they've waited this long.'

'I'm sure. We've talked about it before. She knows me so well... we'd run away and do it on our own, even, but that wouldn't be fair.'

Connie glanced across at her son. 'Sally's definitely the right woman for you,' she said.

Chapter 24

The next few days were a hive of activity. Seb didn't get the chance to go and see Maurice as he'd intended, though he spoke to him on the phone. He also managed to put in motion the plans to buy the property, though it would be into the New Year before anything actually happened.

As usual, everyone was coming to Alec and Connie's for Christmas. Joan had joined them, along with Sally's brother. When Joe and Eve arrived, they said Maurice seemed happy enough, but Seb was determined to see his father. He also brought JP, who'd been fed and changed, so was very content.

Maurice was sitting in the shade out the front of the house, with a book perched on his knee and a glass of water beside him. He started in surprise when Seb pulled up. Seb was pleased by how much better he looked.

'Happy Christmas, Maurice. I've brought someone to see you.' Seb lifted the sleepy baby out of his car seat.

'Happy Christmas. I've got no gifts, I'm afraid. I wasn't expecting to see anyone.'

'Don't worry. I haven't either, really, except this.' Seb passed Maurice a small package. With shaking hands, he unwrapped it. Inside was a framed photo of Seb, Sally and JP.

Maurice was overwhelmed. 'I don't normally get any presents at Christmas... this is just wonderful. Thank you so much.

I'll treasure it for as long as I have left.' He stood and awkwardly put his arms around Seb and baby JP. Then Seb pulled up a chair and they chatted companionably for a short time.

'After New Year's, I'll return to Sydney,' Maurice said. 'When I was in Ipswich Hospital, the doctors there were in touch with mine. I should've gone back before. They can't do much, but my drugs want updating. They gave me a lecture here at the hospital. Besides, I've done what I wanted to do – made peace with Connie and seen you, as well as my grandson. It's been far beyond my wildest dreams. There's only one thing now that I would've liked to have seen.'

'What's that?'

'I'd have loved to have seen you with a horse. To have seen you work this magic I've heard about.'

'Well, Mum's horse is here. We can go and see him if you'd like.'

'No, I mean a horse that's bad, like I've read about.'

Seb scratched his head. 'Nothing's come up yet, since I've just returned and everything's been chaotic. The best I can do is send you a video if something turns up. But I won't really get going again until we have our place up and running.'

'You're going to buy it, then?'

'Yes, it's all in hand.'

JP started to stir.

'I'd better get back,' Seb said. 'This little chap wants feeding.' He got to his feet and embraced Maurice.

Maurice watched him go, and for the first time in his life, he experienced true contentment.

For the family gathered at the Proctors', it was a wonderful day. It was the first Christmas Seb had spent with them in six years. Joe and Eve had missed the last two, and Sally was a new addition, along with her mother and brother and baby. Sarah couldn't be with them, as she had to work, but she'd arrive before New Year's Eve. Caitlin and Bob's children were old enough to be very excited, and Connie revelled in having children around at Christmas. The day flew by in a whirl of eating, playing with the children, and unwrapping presents.

Early the next morning, Connie, Alec, Seb, Sally and JP took a picnic to Haigh Park to relax and enjoy the views. Sally was delighted with the ambience of the place, as she hadn't been before. Joan had returned north to fulfil some commitments, and Eve had phoned to tell Seb that his father seemed very relaxed and happy; she was aware Seb felt a kind of responsibility towards him.

The Christmas break passed by. Seb was itching to get on with his various projects, but first insisted that he and Sally go into Brisbane. He said they needed to look at furniture and appliances for their house. 'But aren't we going to wait until we've bought the place and done it up?' Sally asked.

'Well, I thought we could order stuff now, while the sales are on. Come on, Sal. Mum's dying to look after JP, and it'll be good to have a day to ourselves.'

Sally was nervous about leaving JP after last time. However, she agreed in the end, and they set off. When they got there, Seb headed straight for the jewellery shop. 'I thought we were shopping for household stuff?' Sally asked.

'This is more important to me. I want to show the world how much I love you. You saved me all those years ago, and you've lit up my life now too. This is the least I could do.'

'Oh, Seb, you've saved me too. I missed you so much these last years. Thank goodness we found each other again.'

Sally was shocked by how much Seb assured her he was happy to pay. He told her how much he'd sold the property in England for, and she gasped. 'I didn't realise I was marrying a rich man!' she said.

'It'll soon be a rather poorer one, by the time I've brought that place and done all I want to do. I think we can get away with not having a mortgage. Anyway, you're part of this, so we'll go through all that together.'

They had a very happy day, and fortunately, the ring Sally chose fitted her perfectly; she spent the rest of the trip admiring it. They also bought wedding rings for each other. Seb had planned to find a celebrant as soon as they returned home, but they got back much later than they'd anticipated.

The next morning, they realised it was only three days before New Year's. However, after a series of frustrating phone calls, Seb found a celebrant who would marry them in two weeks. That gave them time to organise everything.

Seb was feeling guilty that he hadn't been to see his father again, though they'd spoken on the phone. On New Year's Eve, he, Sally, and JP set off to see Maurice. They found him in the kitchen with Eve and Joe, having a cold drink and chatting. Seb was again struck by how much better Maurice looked.

After a bit of conversation, Maurice said, 'Now, I have to tell you that I'm returning to Sydney next week. I—'

'No, you can't,' Seb interrupted. 'Sal and I are getting married the following week, and I want you to be there.'

'I told you Seb would say that,' Eve said.

Maurice opened his mouth to protest, but Sally jumped in. 'I want you there too, Maurice,' she said quietly.

Maurice's eyes filled with tears. 'After all the terrible things I did?'

'Yes, well, I was very upset, and as angry as I've ever been – but if everyone else can put up with you, especially Connie, then so can I.'

Maurice sat at the kitchen table, trying to get his emotions under control.

'That's settled, then,' Seb said. 'You're coming. We're having the ceremony at home, so it'll be a very simple and quiet affair.'

'But how will Alec feel? After all, he's more a father to you than I have ever been.'

'I talked to Dad. He's alright with it. He's been the most wonderful father anyone could wish for, and he knows it would mean a lot to me to have you there. Mum also said she understands.'

Maurice gave a rare smile. 'Seems I'm outnumbered, then,' he said.

***

Ten days later, on a beautiful summer day, Seb and Sally were married. Sally wore a simple cream dress and carried a bouquet of pale pink roses. Seb looked handsome in a pink tie that matched her flowers. The white of his shirt made his deep brown eyes stand out, and his hair curled round his ears and collar. They were an arresting couple, Maurice thought, as he looked on from the side of the aisle, watching how they were gliding rather than walking.

On his arrival, he'd been welcomed by some but not by others. Yet he was happy he was here to experience this, even from the sidelines. He observed how proud Alec looked as he took Sally down the aisle. Seb took her hand with a huge smile on his face. The actual ceremony was over very quickly. Then the newlyweds said a few words they'd written themselves, and there wasn't a dry eye anywhere. Even Maurice found himself choking up a little.

The day flew by. The evening was beautiful, with lanterns placed around the garden. Maurice sat in the shadows, watching the proceedings, and thought that this day had been the best of his life.

Alec came and sat beside him. 'How're you going, mate? Are you okay?'

'Yeah. I was just thinking what a great job you've done, raising Seb.'

'I fell for Con as soon as I saw her. Never thought I had a chance, so it wasn't hard to look after both her and Seb, especially when I learnt the circumstances. I couldn't have loved him any more, even if he'd been my own. I'm so proud of the man he's become.'

Maurice nodded. 'I'm sorry about that mower.'

'The old man reckoned you didn't pay him to use his ute, so I gave him fifty bucks.'

Maurice snorted. 'I paid him well, both before and after. Crafty bastard!'

Alec chuckled. 'I rather thought he was having me on.'

Gradually, as the evening progressed, people drifted away. Eventually, there were only Connie, Alec, Sally, Seb and JP left.

Alec got to his feet and pulled Connie up. 'Right, we'll leave you to it. Got everything, Con?'

'Yes, I'm ready.'

'What do you mean?' Seb asked. 'What are you doing?'

'Well,' Connie said, 'you said you wouldn't go away, so Dad and I are going to stay the night in a hotel and leave you lovebirds the run of the place. So, enjoy!'

Connie and Alec gave them both a hug, and away they went.

Seb and Sally looked at each other, then Sally burst out laughing. 'Your parents are priceless, Seb! They think of everything.'

That was reinforced a little while later, when they got to their bedroom. They found the bed covered in red roses and a big bottle of champagne sitting in an ice bucket.

Needless to say, they made the most of it.

Chapter 25

There was a buzzing noise. Seb opened one eye blearily. Was it a fly? No, it was his phone, vibrating by the bed. He groaned and reached out for it, but the call ended. He didn't bother to see who it was. Turning over, he gathered the still-sleeping Sally into his arms and drifted off again.

A little while later, the phone began buzzing again. Sally was disturbed this time.

'Seb, someone wants you,' she muttered.

Seb opened his eyes. As soon as he saw Sally lying naked beside him, he forgot all about the phone.

They were showering together when JP started to demand attention. As Sally got out of the shower to see to him, Seb's phone started to vibrate again. 'Seb, it must be important. Your phone's ringing again.'

Rather begrudgingly, Seb took the phone and saw there were five missed calls. It wasn't a number he recognised, though, so he got dressed and went into the kitchen.

The phone rang again.

'Seb? Seb, is that you? I've been trying to reach you – I rang your dad, and he gave me your number. I need your help!'

'Hang on, who is this?' Seb thought he recognised the voice but couldn't be sure who it was.

'My name's Jim,' the man said, sounding panicked. 'I worked for your dad some years ago.'

'What's wrong?'

'My wife's horse is injured, and we can't get close to help her. She's like a mad thing. We heard you were back, and I thought you'd be the best bet. The vet can't get near her. He said he could dart her with a tranquiliser, but Meg's horrified by that thought. The mare's valuable, and—'

'Where are you?' Seb interrupted. After receiving the directions, he said, 'I'll be there. Hang on.'

Sally came into the kitchen carrying JP. Seb quickly explained that he needed to go.

'I understand, darling,' she said. 'Take care.'

Seb got to the door, then turning back, he said, 'Ring Maurice for me, and ask him if he wants to come. If he does, I'll be there in ten minutes to pick him up. If he doesn't, let me know, and I'll keep going.'

'Why...' Sally started to say, but Seb was gone.

Ten minutes later, Seb drew into his grandparents' place, and sure enough, Maurice was waiting for him.

'This is great,' Maurice said, as he got into the car. 'I'll get to see you in action after all! I really need to get back to Sydney, or so the doctors tell me. We've just had a lockdown. It's lucky you've already had the wedding, though I suppose as it was only family, it wasn't so bad. I worry about crossing the border.'

'Well, let's hope they get on with vaccinations. Then we won't have all these restrictions. At this rate, the mental health issue is going to be greater than the virus.'

Maurice nodded. He knew he was on borrowed time in any case, so in a strange way, he was ambivalent about it all. 'Tell me where we're going and what's happened.'

'I don't know the details yet. We'll be there in a minute, so we'll soon find out.'

Seb turned up a long track, and they eventually came to a house. Beyond it, several people were standing around a yard.

Jim, whom Seb recognised, came rushing up. Seb was focused on the yard, where the mare was. She was a beautiful creature, though her coat was streaked with dirt and sweat. A long, deep gash ran along her flank, along with other smaller cuts. The gash was bleeding quite heavily every time she moved. She had no halter on. If anyone approached the yard railings, she started to rush about, tossing her head. She was clearly nervous and distressed.

Jim's wife, Meg, ran across to Seb too.

'She was in the top paddock under the cliff face, and she must've had a fall,' Meg said, through her tears. 'We found her like this. When we tried to catch her, she panicked and ran into a small gulley, then went down again, hurting herself more. She's cut both knees badly too. We couldn't get near her, though we managed to drive her into the yard.'

'Stay here, everyone,' said Seb. He walked to the fence and climbed through. The mare, who was on the opposite end of the yard, watched him. She snorted loudly and started pawing the ground. Seb stood still, talking in a low, singsong voice. None of the watchers could hear what he was saying, but the mare could. She stopped pawing and stared at him. Standing stock-still, he continued to whisper to her.

After a few more minutes, he took a couple of steps closer. She snorted again but didn't move. All the time, he was talking to her, and her ears were going back and forth. It was plain she was listening to him. He moved forward, step by step, until he was near enough to hold his hand out to her.

The mare tossed her head, then stretched out and sniffed his palm. Slowly, he moved to rub her nose then her forehead. She relaxed and put her head against him. With his arm under her neck, he gently guided her across the yard, then held out his other hand.

'Give me her halter,' he whispered. Meg handed it through the bars. Everyone held their breath. Slowly, Seb put the halter on the horse, who was now compliant, though she still looked nervous. The onlookers clapped, and she threw up her head again and tugged at the rope.

'Quiet,' Seb said. 'She isn't completely relaxed yet.'

He spent several more minutes standing with her, talking gently and stroking her nose, until she relaxed once more.

Seb spoke to the vet. 'Do you want to examine her here or in the stable?'

'With the way she is, let's try here.'

'Come through the gate, then. I'll stay with her while you examine her.'

The vet walked carefully to the mare. Seb kept talking to her and stroking her, and she allowed him to look over her wounds. Apart from the big gash, she had several smaller wounds, and her knees too were a worry. She was now so relaxed that she almost could've been asleep.

'I think you can look after her now,' Seb said to Meg, who was standing nearby. 'She's settled; you won't have any more trouble.' He handed her the lead rope.

'I don't know how to thank you. That was so wonderful, and—'

Seb cut in. 'No thanks necessary. If you need me again, you know where I am. But she'll be right now. She had a bad fright, that's all.' He walked across to Jim and Maurice. 'Ready to go?' he asked his father.

'How much do we owe you?' Jim asked. 'That was incredible.'

'Nothing, it's on the house. I got married yesterday, so if

you'll excuse me, I'll get back to my wife.' As he said this, Seb experienced a real thrill. *His wife!* He couldn't wait to see her.

Maurice didn't speak until they were out on the road again.

'That was one of the most extraordinary things I've ever seen. How did you do it, and what were you saying? We couldn't hear the words.'

'Just telling her that she was okay and I wasn't going to hurt her. Nonsense, really. It's more the tone and cadence of my voice that they like. That was easy – some horses take longer to trust me.'

'Well, I think it's incredible, and I feel so proud of you. I know maybe I have no right to, but I do.'

'Thank you.'

'I plan to leave for Sydney in a couple of days. Will you come and say goodbye? I'd like to see Sally and my grandson before I leave.'

'Sure, we will.'

When Seb got back, Sally was very pleased to see him. 'We're supposed to be on our honeymoon, and here you are, gallivanting after horses!' she teased him. 'We have so much going on... buying that place, overseeing the improvements, getting the land how we want it. We'll have to think of a name, won't we?'

'We already have names. You're Mrs Sebastian Proctor!'

Sally giggled. 'So I am. No, I meant the place we're buying.'

By this time, however, Seb was nuzzling her neck, and all thoughts of names fled their minds. Then they heard a car.

'I hope we haven't returned too quickly,' said Connie, after coming in and seeing them cuddling.

'Since this husband of mine has been out and about this morning, no, not at all.'

Connie looked worried. 'Why, where have you been?'

While Sally made drinks, Seb told Connie and Alec about where he'd gone and why. He also said he was going to say goodbye to Maurice the next day. 'He'd like you to come too, Sal.'

'Of course I will.'

Connie sat looking pensive, then turned to Alec. 'How would you feel if I went too?' she asked.

It was Alec's turn to look thoughtful. Finally, he said, 'I think you should, Con. From what I understand, he hasn't got much time left. If you don't, I think you'll regret it later.'

So it was agreed for the next day.

Chapter 26

The following morning, Seb, Sally, Connie and JP set off to farewell Maurice. They all knew it was going to be difficult, given his illness, as well as the way things were with the lockdowns and border closures. When they arrived, they could see Maurice was very near leaving, though he wasn't going until the next morning.

'I intend to leave very early tomorrow,' he said, by way of explanation. If he was surprised to see Connie, he made no comment. Eve came out from the house with cake and biscuits.

'I have to leave, else I'd become as big as a house,' quipped Maurice.

For her part, Connie was feeling nervous. She didn't know how to conduct herself and sat back, watching the others chat away. Seb was busy regaling Maurice with the expansion plans he had, telling him how they were trying to decide on a name.

Suddenly, Sally said, 'What about Bergerac Horses? After all, that's where we met again.'

'No, I was thinking more along the lines of something like Redeem or Rectify.'

'Both those names sound silly,' said Connie. 'What about Horse Heaven?'

Maurice smiled. 'I'm sure you'll come up with something good. Live there for a bit, get the work done, and the name will come.'

It was time to say goodbye. They had all, in their different ways, been dreading it, though they'd known it was inevitable. Sally was the first to go to Maurice.

'Take care.' She was holding the sleeping baby in her arms, and Maurice bent to give him a quick kiss on the forehead. Sally pecked his cheek and went to the car.

Connie was next, and after a moment's hesitation, she gave Maurice a brief hug. 'Look after yourself,' she whispered. Maurice had been determined to stand strong, but Connie's unexpected hug undid him, and tears flooded his eyes.

'You too,' he said.

Turning to Seb, he opened his arms, and the two men hugged long and hard. Both had tears running down their faces. As Seb released Maurice, he just said, 'Dad.'

Maurice watched them go and squared his shoulders. That last word from Seb meant far more to him than he would've ever believed possible. He felt as if he'd been blessed.

That evening, he said a sad goodbye to Eve and Joe. They'd been very good to him. They hadn't imposed on him and had let him come to them if he wanted company. Eve had fed him well, and he looked much better than he had when he'd arrived. He left soon after midnight, as he thought it would be easier to leave if he couldn't see the beauty of the countryside. He'd realised that he'd fallen in love with this part of Queensland. He knew he'd never come back and had to focus on the next few weeks.

It was strange, he reflected, as he drove. When he'd been told his time was nearly up, he hadn't cared that much. His only aims had been to explain things to Connie and see his son. He'd thought that if he fulfilled those objectives, he would die content. Now, he wanted to live longer, to see his grandson grow, to see his son turn his property into a successful establishment.

He shook himself. He was lucky in so many ways. Regrets

were a waste of time, and Sydney beckoned.

Seb, too, was sad but focused on the future. There was so much to do. The sale had gone through very quickly, but he had to find builders to renovate the place. The power was on, as it had never been taken off. There were an old table and chairs in the kitchen but nothing much else. Maurice had been sleeping in his swag and making do with everything. He'd used a camp oven or open fire to cook with – not that he'd done much of that, Seb thought. He'd effectively been camping there, although he'd paid rent.

Seb and Sally spent days planning the house's furniture and décor. They were having the house extended, so it would have three bedrooms instead of two, as well as an ensuite bathroom, a very large open-plan living area, a modern kitchen and a big deck. It was all planned to retain the charm of the original house. Once the basics were in place, Seb announced he was leaving the rest to Sally, as he was keen to plan the horses' accommodation and training area.

They still hadn't come up with a name. They kept talking of it but couldn't agree. Then one morning, Sally said, 'What was your place in England called?'

'Waterfall Farm Equestrian Centre. Why?'

'That's such a pretty name. Why not use it again?'

'I don't know, really. I didn't think it suited the place.'

'It's not that far to Queen Mary Falls, and there's nothing with a name like that around here. What about Waterfall Farm Retraining Centre?'

'I like that, my clever wife. Now, how about we move in? I know there's lots to do still, but we at least have plumbing and electricity. What do you think?'

'Great idea. I love your mum and dad, but it's time we had our own space.'

About a month after Maurice left, Seb had a phone call from

Brianna. She was very distressed. Her father had contracted the virus and died very quickly. It'd happened a few weeks after Christmas, but she hadn't felt strong enough to speak to Seb until now. She and her brother were taking over the vineyard, though she was hoping to keep riding whenever possible. It was a very sad conversation, and they promised each other to stay in contact.

Time marched on. JP was growing like mad. Seb was busy, as his reputation had spread. Requests for help were soon coming in. Although the place wasn't completed, Seb let a couple of horses come up from New South Wales and put up a temporary yard. Then rumours started to circulate that there was to be a lockdown and the borders would shut again, as there'd been an outbreak of the new Covid variant in NSW.

By the beginning of June, JP was a bonny bouncy baby. His hair was growing much darker. His eyes were also dark; he was going to look like his father.

Then, one morning, Sally was very sick. Towards the end of the day, she perked up, and by dinner time, she was feeling okay. Then, the next morning, she was sick again.

'What's up, Sal?' Seb asked, worried. 'Should you see the doctor?'

Sally shook her head. 'I think I might be pregnant again. I told you it might happen. We don't seem to have a problem making babies, do we? And we did have a good time at Easter!'

Seb gave an enormous smile. 'We did!'

Connie had looked after JP, while Seb and Sally had had two days away at O'Reilly's, up in the mountains. Alec and Connie had insisted they go away, as they hadn't had a honeymoon and had been working very hard getting their place ready.

'They're going to be very close in age, but hopefully that'll be a good thing,' he said.

Sally laughed. 'Oh, Seb! Are you the same man who didn't

want a relationship and certainly didn't want children?'

Seb picked Sally up and swung her round. 'You bet. I don't mind how many kids we have. The more the merrier!'

Sally rushed off to throw up again. Being swung about had made her feel very sick. *Alright for you to say, Seb,* she thought, as she retched.

'You're going to have a brother or sister,' Seb told JP, who just looked at his dad with a big grin. 'Sal, do you mind if I tell Mum and Dad?' he called.

'No, it's okay. Will you tell Maurice?'

Seb still rang his father from time to time. Maurice was always careful with how much he told Seb about his illness, though Seb had realised that they didn't mention it.

That evening, Seb called Maurice, only to find that his phone was switched off. He tried again several times, without success. He worried about it when he went to bed, though Sally pointed out that Maurice had likely just forgotten to charge it. That had happened before.

The next morning, he tried again, but it still went straight to voicemail. Now he got really worried. He kept trying all day, to no avail.

That night, Sally said, 'Look, Seb, I could ring Christopher if you'd like. He's the only link we have to Maurice.'

The only number Sally had was for Christopher's personal phone, so it was a couple of days before he answered. Two days in which Seb worried and they watched the virus spread again through greater Sydney. There was also controversy about the different vaccines; in Queensland, they were telling people under sixty not to have the most easily available vaccine, because they might develop a blood clot – even though it was far less likely to happen than a car accident. Eve and Joe had both been vaccinated, but Connie and Alec hadn't managed it yet, which was frustrating them.

Eventually, Christopher rang Sally back. 'Hello, Sally, how are you?'

Sally paused. It was the first time she'd spoken to him since finding out he'd led Maurice to them. She wasn't sure how she felt about it, but now didn't seem the time to bring it up.

'I'm well. Do you have any news of Maurice?'

Christopher, of course, knew Sally had married her man, and he wished her well. He'd learnt more from Maurice too and knew she was very happy.

'Look, this is hard, but Maurice is in palliative care. He didn't want me to tell you – he didn't want Seb to go and see him – but I told him that you two were worried, and that in the scale of things, you needed to know.'

Sally went pale. 'Oh, no. We were ringing with good news, too. I'm expecting again, and we wanted to tell him.'

Seb was hovering at Sally's shoulder.

'I'll put Seb on,' she said.

The two men had never spoken, and both felt slightly awkward. 'Seb here,' Seb said, rather unnecessarily.

'Seb, yes. Well, as I was just telling Sally, Maurice is very weak. The end is near, I'm afraid.'

Seb had already worked that out from the conversation Sally had been having. He'd known it was coming, but it was still difficult to hear.

'Will you tell him he's going to be a grandfather again and give him our love? Where is he?'

'I've promised not to tell you. He doesn't want you to come charging down here, especially now we're back in lockdown. If you came, then had to quarantine, it wouldn't be good. He remembered you telling him how hard you found it before. It would be even worse for you this time around, now Sally's expecting again.'

'True, but—'

'He was adamant on this. The best I can do is get him to speak to you on the phone; he might agree to that. I'll do my best to persuade him.'

Sally could see conflicting emotions cross Seb's face. In the end, he said, 'Well, I don't want to put you in a difficult situation. Thank you. We'll wait to hear from you.'

After ending the call, Seb sat down at the kitchen bench and rubbed his face. Sally had seen him do this before and knew he was fighting his feelings. She sat down beside him and stroked his back. 'You okay?'

'Not really. I feel a mixture of things, I suppose. I'm glad I got to meet Maurice and that we parted on good terms. I'm sad not to see him again. I told you about Marj and her brother, didn't I?'

'Yes, you said they fell out, then he had Covid and died.'

'She was beside herself. She'd always thought they'd make up one day, but it was too late. I've thought a lot about that lesson lately. Poor Marj... she's a salt-of-the-earth type person but a bit mixed up too.'

'In what way?'

Again, Seb decided to delay telling Sally about Marj getting into his bed. 'This pandemic threw her into turmoil. It was hard for her to find another job, but I got her one in the end.'

Sally hugged him. 'I bet you're a good boss, and all the women love you.'

Seb snorted. 'You're the only one I love. They're wasting their time.'

'Oh, so it's true, then!'

'What? No, I didn't mean that. I meant—'

Sally gave him a playful punch. 'I'm pulling your leg, silly.'

Two days later, Chris messaged to tell them he'd set up a video call with Maurice in the early evening.

Seb and Sally crowded round the computer in Seb's office. Sally had JP on her lap. Though they'd expected it, they were shocked when they saw Maurice; he was unrecognisable. There was no flesh left on him. He was propped up in the bed, with a tube in his nose and an oxygen mask over his mouth.

For a moment, Seb's throat was too tight to speak.

'Hello,' he managed. 'We wanted to tell you some good news. You're going to be a grandfather again.'

With a shaking hand, Maurice removed his mask and whispered, 'How good is that? Keep up the good work with the horses too. Sorry I can't talk more.' This was all said with large spaces between the words, as he was finding it difficult to draw in air.

'That's okay, you just listen.' Seb told him about all the work they'd done and the name they'd decided on for the place. A nurse replaced Maurice's mask. He just nodded and put his thumb up. Then his head tilted back, and he seemed to fall asleep. The nurse told Seb and Sally that he'd had enough for now, but they could maybe have another session in a day or so.

When they shut the computer down, Seb was very upset.

That night, the phone went at 2 a.m. It was Christopher, with the news that Maurice had passed away. He hadn't regained consciousness since he'd spoken to them. Sally got out of bed and made them hot chocolates, putting a small slug of whisky in both. They sat side by side, sipping their drinks.

'You've put some whisky in this, haven't you?' Seb asked.

'Yes, I opened the bottle someone gave us after Christmas. I think it was from the guy whose horse wouldn't let the vet near.'

'That's the last time Maurice and I were together. It's funny, in a way... this time last year, I didn't know anything about him.

Then we met and suddenly, it was better – not okay, but better. I think I'm glad Maurice found peace. How could I hate him when he gave me life?'

Sally leant her head on Seb's shoulder. 'You were pretty stuffed up by it all, though, weren't you? With all that about not wanting children and splitting up with me.'

'True, but look at me now. Soon-to-be dad of two. Most of it's down to you, Sal. You're wonderful, and so full of love and understanding.' Seb put his mug down and kissed Sally tenderly. 'I really am a lucky man.'

The next day, Christopher rang again. 'Look, I feel bad saying this, but Maurice could see the way things were headed with the virus, so he put me in charge of his affairs. He told me categorically that under no circumstances were you to come south of the border. About three weeks ago, he had me make a short video, which he said contained his last wishes. When you've seen it, we'll talk again, though I'm very busy with everything just now – it'll be a few days before I ring again. It's a madhouse down here, and they say it'll only get worse.'

A short time later, Seb and Sally settled in to watch the video.

Maurice was propped up in bed. He looked much the same as he had during their video call. His voice was barely more than a whisper, and he had to stop and collect himself every few words.

'Hello, Seb. I want to make it clear that you're not to come down here to see me or attend my funeral.' Slowly, he shook his head. 'I can imagine you'll think it your duty, but you've done more than enough for me. The bulk of my estate is going to a mental health charity, which Dr Chris will arrange. He'll also send a few personal effects to you.'

He paused, staring into the middle distance.

'There's a ring I've always had... it belonged to my mother, I believe. Please give it to Connie. I think it's valuable. My watch is a good one, too, and I'd like you to have it, then pass it on to JP. There are a few other bits and pieces. Do as you will with them.'

Taking a wheezing breath, he refocused on the camera, his eyes wet.

'I couldn't be prouder of the son I didn't deserve to have. You're the only good thing to come out of my life. When you see this, I'll be gone and finally free from pain, physical and otherwise. Take care, my dear son. I love you.'

It was very painful and disjointed, and Seb and Sally were both crying at the end. Just watching the effort Maurice had needed to put into that little speech was very hard. After a time, Sally got up and made them a hot drink each, and they sat and talked over Maurice's message.

'I'm glad you're not going down to Sydney, Seb. The Covid numbers there keep growing. Imagine if you went, then couldn't get back because they'd closed the border.'

'Shutting the border seems to be the only thing they ever do. Why the hell is it taking so long to vaccinate? Why aren't they thinking of other options? Should we spend the rest of our lives hiding in whichever state we're in? They say we have to live with this thing, but it seems as if they won't allow us to. They don't care about people at all – just about their political points.'

Sally took his hand. 'I agree totally. Just think of how awful it must be for people with close family overseas. If you come into the country, you have to quarantine even if you've had the jab. Many won't be able to afford that.'

A fortnight later, after Maurice's funeral had taken place, a security firm rang Seb and asked for his details, as they were bringing his father's effects. Seb and Sally were surprised by this. Surely, the post would've done. After another three days, a van arrived, and Seb had to sign several forms. The driver then unloaded a big packing case and handed Seb an envelope.

When he opened it, Seb found that it contained two letters, one from Christopher and one from Maurice. He asked the men if they'd like anything before they left.

'We had to get a pass to come here, and it states quite clearly that we're to return straight away,' one said. 'I think we'd better go. The border isn't far, and I want to get this stupid thing over with. One country, are we? Sure doesn't feel like it!'

After they'd gone, Seb and Sally stood looking at the packing case.

'I was expecting a small package with the ring and watch, not all this!' Sally said.

'I'll open the letters first and see what they say,' Seb said.

Christopher's was quite brief.

Dear Sally and Seb,

You'll be surprised to see this amount of stuff, but Maurice was something of a collector, it seems. The charity he selected will receive a substantial amount from the sale of his furniture and apartment. I don't know what's in the packing case. I hope it's not a disappointment, though somehow, I don't think it will be.

Best wishes,

Christopher.

Seb noted how he'd put Sally's name first and remembered how he had been keen on Sally. Seb grinned at her. 'Bit like Christmas, isn't it? Now I'll read Maurice's.'

My dear son,

I hope you don't mind my calling you that. It gives me such joy just to write those words. You'll find a few paintings I've picked up over the years; some are quite valuable, I think. There are also some photos, my journals, and a small, locked box, which contains my watch and my mother's ring. Its key is taped inside the last journal.

You connection with horses is extraordinary. I hope you continue to enjoy it and make many horses into better animals.

This has taken me a few days to write, as I'm struggling. Don't be sad, however. I've done what I set out to do.

Your loving and proud father,

Maurice Windemere.

Seb choked up as he read the last few lines aloud to Sally. She put her arms around him and gave him a cuddle. Once he'd recovered, they opened the packing case. Sure enough, there were paintings cushioned in bubble wrap – landscapes and portraits and modern art. Looking to see who the artists were, Seb recognised some of the names and shook his head, shocked.

'These must be copies or prints,' he said. 'They can't be the real deal.'

The journals were many and varied. Seb put them to one side, planning to read them later. He admired the watch. *I'll only wear it on special occasions,* he thought. The ring was in a small drawstring bag, and both he and Sally gasped when they saw it. It was a dark blue sapphire set in a rose gold band, surrounded by tiny black opals, which looked like sparks of fire when they caught the light.

'I think it's one of the most beautiful rings I've ever seen,' said Sally.

'I wonder what Mum and Dad will think of it,' said Seb. 'How could Maurice afford all of this? You don't think it's stolen, do you?'

'Somehow, I don't. You may find a clue in the journals – and don't forget, Maurice always lived frugally and had no dependants.'

Seb peered into the box again and saw an old envelope. Inside was a photo of his mother, sitting on her horse, speaking to a small group of people. Studying it closely, Seb gasped. 'There's Dad, look, talking to Mum! He was backpacking, exploring, just bumming around, when he and a few other blokes started working for the national parks to earn a bit of money. That's how he met Mum. She'd seen him a few times and liked him. He was actually the one who found her unconscious... Maurice must've taken this.'

Later that night, Seb looked at the journals. There were twenty altogether, and the first started when Seb would've been about two years old. In some ways, he was disappointed, as they just seemed to be about Maurice's job working security in mines. As Seb flicked through them, he realised Maurice had ended up working in some of the most remote and dangerous places in the world, with his own security team – maybe even his own company. Most of it was very factual, about shifts and employment. Personal thoughts and feelings were hidden from the reader. Even the few skirmishes he'd been caught in were described in a way that made them almost boring. Clearly, he'd always been a very private man. Reading the journals, he seemed unemotional, though Seb knew that wasn't the case.

The next day, Seb took the ring over to his mother. Connie's eyes widened when she saw it.

'It's so beautiful, Seb, but I don't want it,' she said. 'Give it to Sally. If the next baby is a girl, she should have it.'

They were both silent for a bit with their own reflections on the complexity of Maurice's character, then Seb roused himself.

'Better get back. I'm glad I didn't go down to Sydney, as I would've been trapped. I don't think I could've taken another fortnight in quarantine. There'll be more people with mental illness than with Covid, the way things are shaping up. Don't think the supposed leaders know what they're doing.'

Driving back to his little family and his new business, Seb was suddenly overcome with optimism. It'd been a cold start to the day, as it was winter, but the sun was shining out of a clear blue sky. He had a wife he adored, a lovely son, and another child on the way, as well as three horses expected to turn up the next day. He was much luckier than the thousands who relied on tourism or had food outlets.

Again, Seb wondered about the man who'd fathered him. He'd only scratched the surface of his personality, but it no longer mattered that there were things he didn't know. He knew enough.

Though the world was changing, he was truly happy. At that moment, he knew he would cope with whatever was thrown at him over the coming years. With his wife, children, and horses, he'd be alright. Pandemic, fire, flood – whatever happened, it didn't matter. He was strong; he was a survivor.

Also by Gillian Wells

Children's Books
The Amazing Adventures of Bub and Tub Volume One
The Amazing Adventures of Bub and Tub Volume Two

Adult Fiction
Alone
Consequences

Inheritance

Lost

Shawline Publishing Group Pty Ltd
www.shawlinepublishing.com.au

SLP
SHAWLINE
PUBLISHING
GROUP

More great Shawline titles can be found by scanning the QR code below.
New titles also available through Books@Home Pty Ltd.
Subscribe today at www.booksathome.com.au or scan the QR code below.